TOGETHER
or
Apart

Emmie Beth Manor

ISBN 978-1-0980-3096-4 (paperback)
ISBN 978-1-0980-3097-1 (digital)

Christian Faith Publishing, Inc.
832 Park Avenue
Meadville, PA 16335
www.christianfaithpublishing.com

Printed in the United States of America

I would like to dedicate my first book to those God
used to show me the talent He gave me for writing and
who helped me finish and edit my first book:
Mr. Tony Smith my seventh grade English teacher
who showed me I am a writer, and
the women's writing group from Southern Seminary
who encouraged me to finish this book and read
through the book for first round edits.

CONTENTS

CHAPTER 1

"It is a girl!" exclaimed the midwife, placing the wet, wiggling baby on Mama's chest. Mama grinned with a twinkle in her eye that showed so much love in spite of the labor she had endured. I marveled at this amazing sight, though it scared me greatly. Being seventeen and due to be married in just over a year, Mama decided I should be present for the birth of her tenth child.

"She is so beautiful!" Mama said with tears of joy streaming down her face. Her sisters attended her and helped clean off the baby as the midwife cut the umbilical cord and finished her business. "Look at her, Sarai. Is she not beautiful?"

I could not answer. I could not move. I simply stared in continued amazement at what had just occurred.

"Do not be afraid, my sweet. Come see your sister."

I moved slowly to Mama's side and looked at the new creation that had just entered the world. I had seen many a baby before, even on the day they were born, but it was nothing compared to seeing the actual birth. Seeing the birth causes an absolute wonder at what life really is. I reached my hand to gingerly touch her tiny fingers. "She is beautiful, Mama." I smiled gazing at the babe, lying so still and comfortable on Mama's chest. As I began to process what had happened in the room, I thought a loud, "Papa should be here for this."

"Gracious, child!" exclaimed the midwife. "Birthing new life is the woman's business. Men should not be troubled with such things." She had finished her duties with the after birth and helping Mama to sit up she put the baby to breast. "See," she said after the latch, "men do not understand these things and do not need to be involved in the process."

Mama looked at me with her kind eyes that said we will discuss it another time.

Once the baby finished nursing, my aunts made Mama presentable while the midwife bathed the child and dressed her in a small gown Mama had made. The three women tidied the birthing room so that not a drop of blood or fluid could be seen. After checking Mama one more time, the midwife left to get Papa, who was with the children in the main part of the house.

Papa entered the room on the heels of the midwife and being quite experienced in this, picked up his new daughter and kissed her smooth head, followed by a kiss on Mama's head and a huge grin.

"Is she not beautiful, John?" Mama said tenderly as Papa knelt beside the bed.

"She is a gem, my dear." Papa gave Mama a look I would never forget. So full of love and admiration for the woman he called his own.

"And what shall we call our beautiful little gem?"

"What do you like, darling?"

"I am fond of Magdalene, a faithful follower of Christ, Mary was."

"So it will be. And her second name shall be Joyce, for I rejoice that God has granted us with another child after we thought there would be no more."

"Magdalene Joyce, my precious gem." Mama touched her gently and kissed her soft cheek.

The amount of love that shone on their faces amazed me even further, for the part that was about to come I had been privileged to witness six times prior. But I knew at that moment I had been allowed to see something so special, so intimate, which could only be seen in the birth of the child.

Moments passed as my parents admired the new life in front of them. I do not know how many but I saw Mama give a nod before Papa said, "The children may come now."

Again, the midwife checked on Mama and left to gather my siblings from the house. No time passed before we heard many feet running to the birthing room to see the new baby. Papa held her close as one by one the other children entered. Once all were in, Papa held her up for all to see. "Come meet your sister, Magdalene Joyce!" I took my place behind Josiah and from oldest to youngest we each kissed the babe and Mama and then gathered at the foot of Mama's bed. Papa handed Magdalene to Mama and pulled the family Bible from a shelf where it had been carefully placed when Mama came to her confinement, as labor began. Papa prayed a blessing over Magdalene for her future and read from Psalm 139, in which the Psalmist thanks God for his own life:

> For you formed my inward parts; you knit-
> ted me together in my mother's womb. I praise
> you, for I am fearfully and wonderfully made.
> Wonderful are your works; my soul knows it very
> well. My frame was not hidden from you, when I
> was being made in secret, intricately woven in the
> depths of the earth. Your eyes saw my unformed
> substance; in your book were written, every one
> of them, the days that were formed for me, when
> as yet there was none of them.

Though I had heard Papa read this prayer after many siblings' births, I never tired of it. It was special for the family to celebrate life before the town celebrated later and named her husband-to-be. Yes, you heard me correctly! As babes, we were betrothed and knew for our whole lives who we would one day marry. This may seem odd to many, but for us it was our way of life. I believed it was this way so that we would have time to get used to the other person before we wed, especially since we married at a young age, typically eighteen.

Our town was quite traditional and followed procedure accord- ingly. Everything had its place and everything had its ritual, but com- pared to the rest of our town, our family was different. My parents really did love each other and all of their children. They took the

Bible and Christian life seriously. They wanted all of us to take it seriously. But their seriousness went beyond rigid rules and structure. It was a way of life I had not seen anywhere else.

I do believe my family was the first, with the March family, to alter the betrothal ritual by delaying it. I was betrothed to Matthew March, the oldest son, who is two years my senior. Most are betrothed to someone closer in age, usually by months. But as our parents are best friends, they made an agreement that their oldest of opposite genders would be betrothed; so Matthew's betrothal waited until I was born two years later.

Honestly I did not understand this as the March family was extremely traditional and quite strict in the ways of our ancestors, but so it was.

"I so wish Samuel would have been here," I heard Mama express to Papa after the gathering was complete. "This is the first birth of which he has not been a part."

"I know, Esther, but he will be home in a couple of weeks. I will send a letter to him first thing tomorrow." Papa kissed Mama and took the children back to the house.

Here I should interject that Samuel, the oldest of our family, stepped outside our ways. Though attaining additional education away from our town is considered acceptable, other than Uncle Mark, I know of no one else who has done it, especially since he never came back. Yes, my father's second brother decided to attend university, met an outside woman, and came back only to tell the family he was going to move to the city. Did I mention this is simply not done? He is the only one in the history of the town who has ever done this, and our town has a deep history here. The reason for this is that, if you decide to leave, it is as if you had never been born! The only reason I knew my uncle existed was because my parents did not believe this to be right so, when we were old enough to be trusted, we were allowed into the family secret: my parents still had contact with him. Many people knew of this "shame on our family," but no one knew—especially our grandparents—that Papa corresponded with his brother regularly. And because of Uncle Mark, the whole town was wondering what would happen with Samuel when he returned for Christmas.

"How are you feeling, Mama?" I asked, bringing her some water and clean clothes.

"I am tired but so joyous. Can you believe another girl?" My aunts took the clothes and cleaned up Mama. "You need to hold her, Sarai. You need the practice."

Mama placed the tiny babe in my arms. She was so pink and perfect with beautiful round cheeks, ten fingers and ten toes. In a couple of years, this was likely to be me. I could not imagine, could not fathom the idea of having a family, and yet it was so close.

"Does it always feel like this when you hold a new baby?" I asked Mama.

"What do you mean, Sarai?"

"Like you are, for just a moment, holding a piece of heaven."

"Wait until the baby is yours." My aunts smiled at this. They finished attending to Mama and went into the house to prepare food for their families and us. When Mama saw we were really alone, she asked, "What is on your mind, Sarai? You have seemed a bit troubled since the birth."

I smiled at Mama. God had truly blessed her with mothering abilities. Even in the birth of her tenth child, she was still in tune with her other children. "Oh, Mama, there are so many things on my mind. I do not know where I should begin."

It was Mama's turn to smile. "Choose something, and the rest will come."

I handed Magdalene back to her and sat on the bed. Taking a deep breath, I sighed. "Am I really ready for this life?"

"What do you mean?"

"Am I ready to be a wife and a mother and to run a home? I know it is still a year and a half before the wedding, but it still does not seem like enough time. There is too much to learn. I could never run a home as you do, Mama."

"Never say never, my darling. I used to think the same thing. And by the grace of our Lord, here I am. A wife, a mother of ten beautiful, healthy children, and running a home as the Lord sees fit."

"What about Papa? Why can he not be here for the birth? It seems like he should at least be allowed in the room for the birth."

"Honestly, that comes down to tradition. This is the way it has been and so it stays. There is no right or wrong in this, it just is. Your father would love to be in here for the births but he simply is not allowed."

"And what about Samuel? Is he really going to marry Amelia?"

"Of course he is. How could you ask such a thing?"

"Because of Uncle Mark." My voice softened.

"Oh, sweet girl. Let me explain the difference between Mark and Samuel. When Mark left, he was strong, ambitious, and self-centered. He believed everything the world had to offer was good. He fell for a woman who broke his heart. He tried to come home but was not allowed. He got involved in a church and became a Christian. He married Dianna and is now living a godly life. He has attempted to make amends in vain.

"Samuel, on the other hand, simply wanted to study modern agriculture to find ways to help our town and our farming techniques so hopefully we can produce more and help with local farms nearby. He loves Amelia so much and will be coming back for her. He is also a Christian and has sought the Lord's guidance in every step."

"This is overwhelming, Mama. I have so much to think on, to learn, and to figure."

"What do you mean, dear?"

Here my breath caught. I did not know if I could confess to Mama my greatest fear, the thing that was circling my brain continuously as I watched Mama labor and give birth. Now in her time of joy would I break her heart? I looked in her eyes as small tears welled in mine. "Mama, will I ever love Matthew?"

CHAPTER 2

Just then, the door flew open as my grandparents on Mama's side came into the room with Papa close behind them. Grandma hugged, kissed, gushed, and cooed. Grandpa shook Papa's hand and patted him on the back with congratulations. I stepped back to my place during the delivery to wipe my eyes and pull myself together. Now it would probably be days before I could talk privately with Mama. I saw her nod and Papa told the other children they could come back into the room. Though the room was quite large, it suddenly felt overcrowded. I quietly backed out and went to help my aunts prepare the food. Food for twenty-six after helping with labor is a huge task, but thankfully that was all who would come this night.

The next week was full of friends and family coming to visit, bringing food and gifts as well as suggestions for Magdalene's betrothed. Even in this delicate time, Mama kept her spirit and her composure and graciously accepted everything, including unwanted advice.

Two weeks before Magdalene's birth, a family my parents had great respect for had a baby boy. My brother, Gabriel, was betrothed to their oldest daughter and so this was their primary consideration for Magdalene, though both children had to be at least a month old before it could be officially decided and most waited six, to see the personality of the children. This took off some pressure for Mama as she still had to prepare for Samuel's wedding that would be taking place the day Magdalene turned one month.

As things settled the next week, we began preparations for Samuel and Amelia's wedding. Papa and the boys worked hard on the little house for them on our property. Mama, Tamar, and I finished sewing the family's clothes for the occasion. Amelia came over as often as she could to help and brought her sister and my best friend, Joanna, who also happens to be betrothed to my second brother, Josiah.

I guess I should do a quick explanation about families and betrothals. Family is very important and to help with keeping families together, many times they will marry off several children in the same family to children in another family. There was also a thought that by doing this, it helped in the future selection of husbands and wives so not everyone is directly related to keep things proper. I know this sounds a bit complicated and it is if you are unfamiliar with this way of thinking. When you are brought up in it, however, it is like breathing.

When the girls would come, we would discuss the wedding as we sewed. Mama felt guilty having them at our house instead of making their preparations at their home. But they said Mrs. Safford insisted on the girls helping us. And, after all, Mama had a new baby. With the two of them, we were able to finish most of our clothing in the week before Samuel came home.

In fact we were sitting in the family room sewing some lace onto the girls' dresses when Miriam looked out of the window and screamed, "Papa and Samuel are coming!"

Amelia immediately jumped up and said, "I must go!" Since they had been apart so long, they had decided not to see each other until their wedding day. We bundled her quickly and she and Joanna ran out the back door just as the front one opened. We hurried to the front and acted as if nothing had gone awry.

Children came running from all over the house yelling, "Samuel! You are home!"

But Mama made sure she got to him first. "Look at how much you have grown, my son!" They kissed cheeks and hugged warmly. "I have missed you, Samuel."

"Me too!" said Miriam, pushing for her turn.

Samuel picked her up and said, "It is so quiet without eleven other people around all the time. I have missed you all so much. Now where is my new sister?"

We all hugged him as we walked into the living room where Magdalene slept in her cradle. He lifted her so gently and kissed her forehead. He was ready to be a papa. "I am sorry I missed the big day." All worked ceased for the remainder of the day as we talked and enjoyed being with the whole family.

That evening after I thought everyone was in bed, I heard hushed voices in the kitchen. I discerned Papa, Mama, and Samuel's voices and attempted to tune out the noise as I assumed they were talking about either school or the wedding. I was almost asleep when I heard my name.

"Yes, I think Sarai would enjoy that," Mama said. My eyes widened and my ears perked. I tried to listen but could barely hear their voices.

"There is plenty of room for us all. They would be honored," said Samuel. My stomach turned. I could tell they were talking about the city and possibly something about my uncle, aunt, and cousins.

"I think it best for them to decide." I heard Papa's voice. My mind began to race. What did this mean?

Little did I know I was in for an adventure of a lifetime.

CHAPTER 3

But first came Christmas. A very joyous time in our home and our last family event before Samuel was married. I awoke to the smell of Mama making breakfast and quickly readied myself to go and help her.

"Merry Christmas, Mama!" I exclaimed giving her a big hug from behind.

"Merry Christmas, Sarai!" Mama turned and kissed my cheek with flour all over her hands.

"What can I do?" I asked looking at the biscuits ready to be put over the fire.

"I still need eggs from the hen house. Will you get two dozen?"

"Yes, ma'am." A gentle snow was falling. I put on my boots, sweater, and shawl, and grabbing a basket, I went to the backyard where we kept our animals.

I suppose I need another brief explanation here. I said in the beginning our town is very traditional and, as I am sure you have guessed, more quaint, if you will. Outsiders might call us backward. Similar to Amish or Mennonites, we live off the land. We are farmers that do not use modern technology. We use basic tools and our hands. We do have phones and basic electricity, but we use both very seldom. We use horse and buggies to get around and there are a couple cars kept in case we need to make long travels to take our produce out to cities and towns that are farther out. We build our own homes and barns. Men wear trousers and buttoned shirts. Girls wear skirts, blouses, and scarves. Mostly we just live simply.

When I returned to the home, the house was alive with activity. Tamar was helping Mama with the corn meal and sausage. Papa, Samuel, and Josiah were building a fire. Ezekiel and Gideon were putting dishes on the table and the little ones were playing on the floor.

I hurried the eggs to Mama and then retrieved milk and cheese from the ice box. As the food finished, I set the items on the table and the boys looked quite anxious. Finally Mama gave the "time to eat" signal, and we quickly gathered around the table. Papa blessed the food and thanked God for this wonderful day to celebrate the birth of Jesus. After a hearty "amen" from all, the breakfast feast began.

Once all had their fill, the table was cleared, and we moved to the living area. Papa and Mama sat in their rockers, and we children gathered on the rug by the fire. Papa took the family Bible to read to us. Every Christmas we read the birth of Christ from Luke 2. We all listened intently. I never tire of hearing about the first Christmas along with Papa's yearly explanation of why we give gifts. Papa prayed again for this special day and then handed out the gifts. Our gifts are hand crafted and full of meaning from the heart. This year Mama made a pillow for me that had "Trust in God" cross-stitched on one side. It was beautiful and I did not know then how much I would need this reminder. We all thanked Papa and Mama then began to talk, relax, and play.

Magdalene started fussing. "Sarai, come and help me with the baby," Mama said. I hopped up and followed her back to the birthing room, though it did not dawn on me where we were going. Mama sat on the bed to nurse Magdalene and motioned for me to sit next to her. "So, where did we leave the conversation last time?"

I looked at her puzzled then looked at where she had taken me. "You are talking about my question." I tucked my head.

Mama lifted my chin and looked into my eyes. "There is no reason to be ashamed, my child. All women ask these questions here, though few admit it. We should have a little privacy for a few moments at least." She smiled at me.

My breath caught and the tears began to come and I asked again, "Will I ever love Matthew?"

In her wise way, Mama asked, "Why do you not?"

I shrugged my shoulders and looked down at my hands. "Something this summer has really been bothering me. He is very straight. His family is completely steeped in the tradition of the town. It is not that I do not like our ways, but somehow Papa and you are different. You love each other. You teach the truths of the Bible and live them instead of by rules for the sake of rules. The other families here, especially his, seem like they just want us women to make home and be silent. But Papa honors and loves you. I want that, Mama, and I am not sure I can love someone who is not that way."

Mama continued to smile. She touched my hand. "Matthew is a good man, from a good family. He could be more than you think. And we are called to honor our husbands no matter what they say or do."

And that is when it hit me like lightening. My head snapped up and I looked at Mama right in the eyes. "Mama, does God want me to marry Matthew?"

Mama chuckled. "Have you asked God if He wants you to marry Matthew?"

"No. I have not."

"Then maybe you should."

CHAPTER 4

Four days after Christmas, it was time for the wedding. The house was all a buzz; dressing, combing hair, washing faces and gathering flowers and ties. Samuel looked so handsome and all of us were in our best. We loaded in the wagon as bundled as we could be and headed to the center of town where the ceremony would take place.

Our family gathered on the groom's side of the church and waited in anticipation for the Safford's to arrive. The rest of the invited guests were already present and waiting patiently. Then we heard the wagon. The minister came in from the back and shook Samuel's hand. The Safford family entered looking regal. The children came in from youngest to oldest and Mr. and Mrs. Safford walked on either side of Amelia. She looked so beautiful and elegant in her wedding dress. I wanted to run and tell her so but dared not for two reasons. One, it would have been out of order and would have drawn nasty looks from all. Two, the church believed that out of infancy focusing on beauty and commenting on outward appearance would lead to self-centeredness and vanity. So in silence, I admired the intricate work of her wedding dress and the serenity displayed on her face and being. It was clear by her smile and overall demeanor that she had waited in anticipation to be joined to the man she loved, and my heart ached knowing that I would simply be joined to the man chosen for me with anxiety and dread.

The service was beautiful and simple as the pastor read from the Bible, rings were exchanged and candles lit. When we join in marriage, we are joining two families so unlike the traditional three candles, each person has a candle that light a candle together for each side and then the bride and groom join those two candles together into one flame. It is so beautiful. I love the atmosphere of candle light.

And then they are joined together. Samuel led his bride out of the church and over to the town hall where the joint festivities would take place. Already gathered there was a group of chosen instrumentalists to play traditional folk tunes and hymns. Amelia's aunts were busy preparing the last of the food.

As Samuel and Amelia walked in, the music began for the Wedding Waltz. He took his bride into his arms and danced her around the room. How he learned so well to dance I do not know but he was a wonderful leader on the floor. We all learn folk dances as children but many do not practice later on as we are not allowed to co-ed dance after the age of ten unless it is with a family member. In fact we are not allowed to touch anyone of the opposite gender unless they are family or a child. This was to keep away temptation of that kind until marriage, and as far as I knew, it worked.

After the Wedding Waltz came, the Family Jig where the two families joined on the floor and celebrated the new family created. As the jig ended, Amelia's aunts brought out more food than I thought possible to make. Everyone took their seats at their tables and turned their attention to the couples table. Samuel gave a brief speech of appreciation, sharing what the day meant to them.

"Amelia and I are so blessed to have you in our lives. We are thankful to have such wonderful family and friends to help us celebrate our joining together. We hope you enjoy yourselves! Let us give thanks for the food Amelia's family has prepared." He blessed the food and the meal was served. The aunts had truly out done themselves, and the food was absolutely delicious.

I sat next to Joanna, which thrilled me because of all the happenings the past couple of months we were unable to spend any time talking alone.

"What a wonderful day!" Joanna exclaimed. "Just a year and a half, Sarai, and we will be celebrating." She beamed at me.

My stomach churned and I tried to smile back but it only half came.

"Are you all right?" she asked, looking quite concerned.

I glanced across the room and saw Matthew sitting with his family. My stomach tightened even more as I tried to will the feelings of love and excitement. "I am all right. There is much on my mind right now."

"What is it?" Joanna touched my arm with a look of genuine concern.

I began to tear and blinked quickly to avoid completely losing it. I shook my head and forced a smile.

"I understand." She squeezed my arm. "We will talk New Year's Day." I loved how well Joanna and I knew each other. So many times we only had to say little if anything at all. The music began to play again. "Come, Sarai," Joanna exclaimed suddenly. "Dancing will get your mind in a better mood."

I really smiled and followed her to the dance floor. We danced to the jigs and folk tunes the band played until our legs ached. It was such fun. We broke for some cake and fruit drink, then proceeded back to the dance floor to add more ache to our legs. It felt like hours but it was over all too soon. Samuel and Amelia jumped into their wagon Papa built and took off to their cozy cottage on the north side of the family property. I teared again, but this time I let the water flow, watching them ride down the road in the setting sun looked like something out of a fairy tale.

CHAPTER 5

It was New Year's Eve when we saw Samuel and Amelia again. Amelia had a new glow about her. She seemed genuinely happy in her marriage to Samuel; content to be the wife of her betrothed. The day was splendid as we talked, ate, played, sang, and danced. The little ones were beginning to understand marbles and pick-up sticks. Mama made our typical cornbread, black-eyes peas, and collard greens meal for lunch. We thoroughly enjoyed being together as a family.

After lunch was cleared, the children bundled up to go play outside as Mama commanded they do whenever possible. Once the house was quiet and the children active outside, Papa directed Mama, Samuel, Amelia, Josiah, and me to the family table. My stomach began to flutter. Whenever we were directed as such to the table, we knew something important and/or serious was about to be discussed. Once all were seated, Papa gave Samuel a nod.

"As you two know," Samuel began, "Amelia and I will be heading back to the city so I can study more." He paused. Josiah and I nodded but said not a word. "To finish my studies more quickly, we have decided to stay for the summer and we would like for you to come spend the summer in the city with us."

Both of our mouths dropped in disbelief followed by a look to Papa and Mama. They were smiling and nodding to give their approval. I spoke first. "We are able to spend a whole summer in the city?"

"If you would like, the invitation is there," replied Samuel with a smile.

Josiah looked concerned. "Are you sure about this Papa? Is it really wise?"

"What would make it unwise, Josiah?" Papa asked.

"Given our family history, I am unsure it is a good idea to leave the town. I am surprised you are allowing Samuel to leave again." There was a hint of resentment in the tone.

"But he has returned, married his betrothed and he is a grown man as you have just become. He can choose for himself on what path to lead his family. I believe he is following God's plan for Him at this time. And I have no reservations about any of our family leaving if that is what God chooses for them. My brother may not have made the wisest decisions when he was younger, but God has used it to bring Mark to Jesus and live a life surrendered to Him."

Josiah thought on these words while I boldly declared, "I want to go. I want to see what life is like out there."

Josiah said, "But what will the town say?"

Papa let out a sigh. "Josiah, I have learned to let them talk. Your Mama and I have prayed over this, and we believe this is a great learning and growing opportunity for you both."

"Will Joanna be coming with us?" I asked thinking it would be a great opportunity for her as well.

Amelia laughed. "My parents do not want me to go, but they know I am under my husband's leadership now. They will not even consider letting Joanna go, especially since she is not yet married."

Josiah sat up straighter and puffed out his chest. I giggled. "And that is probably another reason they do not want her to go," said Samuel and we all had a laugh.

"I will speak with Joanna about it," said Josiah. "When do you need a decision?"

"As soon as possible would be best," Samuel responded.

"Then I guess it is good I am seeing her tonight," Josiah smiled with a clear change in mood.

"And you need to speak with Matthew tonight also, Sarai," Papa told me.

I started. I had completely forgotten he would be over to celebrate the New Year that evening. "Yes, Papa," I said with a forced smile. But that is when my mind took off. "Speak with him? About what? We are not yet married and he has no say in this matter. I am going whether or not he approves. This is my time to be out from under all these expectations of being exactly a certain way and away from him. I can truly be free."

For an hour, I stewed in my mind while smiling and talking with my family. My siblings came inside, and Mama, Tamar, and I started working on dinner. The house was alight as the children played on the living room floor. Thankfully, Tamar talked while we cooked, so I was able to think as I worked. I battled with myself, what I wanted to say versus what I actually should say. I did not know what was happening to me. Never had I felt like this. Never, until six months before, had I even questioned the life I was living or what I was supposed to be doing. But something in me was stirring.

A knock at the door caused me to jump and my stomach to churn. Samuel, Amelia, and Josiah had just left to go to the Safford home and I knew who was at the door.

Papa opened it and said, "Matthew, come in son."

"Good evening, Mr. Lindell. It is a cold evening, a great way to start the New Year," said Matthew with a laugh.

My stomach continued to churn and my hands began to shake as I put the corn bread on the fire to bake.

"Sarai, Matthew is here," Papa called to me so I could greet Matthew.

"I will be one minute, Papa. I am putting the bread on the fire." I prayed they could not hear the shaking in my voice. Once the bread was settled on the rack, I checked with Mama who told me to go. I went to the entry way where the men stood. "Good evening, Matthew," I said with a small curtsy.

"Good evening, Sarai," Matthew said, bowing his head.

"May I take your coat?" Matthew removed his coat and placed it on my arms careful not to touch me. "Please come in and have a seat." I directed him to the family room. "Dinner will be ready shortly." He sat and my brothers swarmed him. I breathed a deep sigh and put his coat on the coat rack. I went back to the kitchen to help finish the meal and set the table. I could not figure out why I was so nervous. I had made up my mind; it did not matter what he said.

While dinner was cooking, Tamar and I put out the place settings, then took each platter to the table as they finished. Once everything was ready, Mama called everyone to gather around the table. We took our places, Matthew's being directly across from mine, and joined hands for the blessing. Papa said, "Amen." We sat and immediately began passing the food. There was light chatter until all were served their share. Papa ate quickly and then began the traditional New Year's discussion while the rest of us finished eating.

"What a blessed year it has been for our family!" Papa began. "We were given far more crops than ever before. Magdalene joined our family, a wonderful surprise. And though they are not here this evening we celebrated the joyous marriage of Samuel and Amelia. God has been so good to us. Now let us go around the table and share your favorite memory of the year and what you hope to learn or achieve in the year to come."

I searched my mind for the right words as I knew I could say nothing about the possible summer venture. I waited patiently as each person shared their memories and hopes until it came back to me. "Sarai, please share," Papa said with a look to not mention the summer.

"My favorite memory was being present for Magdalene's birth. What a miracle it was! This year I hope to learn and grow in understanding the plans God has in store for me." I smiled at Papa who smiled back with a thankful nod.

Once all had spoken, Papa concluded our sharing time and Mama brought out a delicious vanilla cake. We all indulged in a small piece. As we finished our dessert, we took our dishes to the kitchen. The boys and little ones went to the living area to play or read. Tamar and I cleared the serving dishes then went to fill the washing bucket at the well. After putting the bucket on the heating rack, Mama excused me to talk with Matthew. Usually it would have been a treat to not wash dishes, but that night I would gladly have taken washing over a discussion of the summer with him.

He was sitting, talking to Papa when I came out of the kitchen. As soon as he saw me, Matthew jumped to his feet and said, "Excuse me, Mr. Lindell. It is time for me to speak with Sarai." Papa smiled. "Come, Sarai." Matthew put his arm out for me to pass. I walked slowly to the courting table at the back of the room. I sat on my side and Matthew on his. He looked into my eyes and smiled. He began by complimenting the dinner, telling me I was learning from the best and that I was going to be a great wife and mother. I wanted to yell, "Stop saying those things!" but I sat in silence waiting for him to finish speaking. "Are you looking forward to classes beginning again?"

The question took me off guard since I had been preparing a speech in my mind, but I realized that he had provided me with an introduction. "Yes, I do enjoy the classroom, but more than that, I am looking forward to the summer." I smiled sweetly at him and he looked puzzled. "I really need to discuss something with you," phrasing it this way simply to be polite.

Matthew's expression turned to concern. "I am listening."

I took a deep breath and looked into his eyes. "Samuel and Amelia have invited Josiah and me to spend the summer with them in the city and I would like to go."

He looked at me for a moment, then smiled, relaxing completely. "Is that all you want to discuss?"

I gave him a funny look and replied, "Yes. Is that amusing?"

"No, I just expected something extremely serious."

"You do not think this is serious?"

"It could be. But I trust your family and you."

It would have felt better if he had slapped me across the face. I was questioning everything and I hear my betrothed say he trusts me! "You do?" I said trying to hide the surprise in my voice.

"Yes. I trust your family more than any other in the town, and I think you should go."

"*What*?" Slap the other cheek! My jaw hit the floor.

He moved in slightly and looked me square in the eyes and said, "I think you should go."

"You are not going to try to dissuade me?"

"Why would I, Sarai? You are going for a summer, not forever. And after we are married there probably will not be a reason for us to go. So take this opportunity and see what else is out there. Since your parents approve, I do as well."

I looked at him at a loss for words, staring at his face for a hint that he was getting my hopes up and would then dash them. But I saw none of that. Who was this man sitting in front of me? "Are you sure?" I said nervously.

He smiled so sincerely. "Yes. Go."

I smiled back, though now, thoroughly confused. "I am amazed by what I am hearing, Matthew. Your family is so in line with the old traditions of our town. From where is this coming?"

Matthew smiled slyly. "I want to tell you, but it will have to wait until another time. The setting is not appropriate." He looked at the children playing in the floor. I understood and nodded. We sat in silence, watching the children play.

My heart pounded with excitement, my head with questions and confusion. "What does this mean?" I thought to myself and mulled over the implications of the conversation.

"Sarai," Matthew broke through the internal dialogue. I looked at him. "Promise me you will write so I can learn about the city, since I will not be able to go. Let me experience it through you."

I nodded at him. "I can do that. It is the least I can do."

As I lay down for bed that evening, I replayed my conversation with Matthew. It was still sinking into my head as it seemed so out of the ordinary for him. I thought again about the implications of his telling me to go. Was he questioning the arrangement too? Did he want to be free? Was he testing me? Only time would tell. I was thankful Matthew wanted me to go, and I began to prepare myself for what the summer might hold.

CHAPTER 6

I awoke early New Year's Day as it was the one day Joanna and I had a day to visit as long as we liked. I helped Mama prepare breakfast and ate with the family. I cleared dishes as quickly as I could and checked with Mama and was given permission to go meet Joanna. I took a couple of blankets, some left over biscuits and some matches and headed to our special place in the woods.

I arrived first and built a small fire to help keep us warm. Joanna came a few minutes later with our quilt and hot cocoa. We embraced, arranged our blankets, and settled in for our annual free day. Per usual, we started with light chat, remembering Christmas day and the festivities of the wedding as well as recapping the year together. Silence then fell between us for a few moments. Both of us knew that that was the signal for the heavier things that we wanted to discuss. I could not decide where to begin, so, unintentionally, Joanna decided for me.

"Sarai," she said in her calm reassuring voice, "I have been concerned about you ever since the wedding. Why did mentioning our weddings cause you such distress?"

Because of the cold, I did not want to cry, but no matter how much I tried to will them away, the tears came without control. "Oh, Joanna," I whispered as I wiped my eyes, "I do not even know." I let the tears flow for a minute and then composed myself. Joanna just held my hand and waited patiently. Finally I said slowly, "I am not sure I want to marry Matthew."

Joanna looked at me with great surprise. "What do you mean, Sarai?"

"I do not love him," I stated matter-of-factly. "During the summer, I began thinking, evaluating our lives, our families. The March family is so strict, so traditional. I do not want to just be the silent wife and mother. I want love, to be cherished, to share ideas. I want a marriage like my parents."

"How do you know it will be that way?"

"Look at his family and tell me it would not be. Everything with them is just so and Mrs. March never speaks around the men. She is this perfect woman. Men expect their wives to be like their mothers and that is not me." I took a breath, thought for a moment, then continued with, "And furthermore, I do not know where he stands in his faith. Since they follow the traditions so closely, my guess is it is religious like most others."

"Have you talked to him about it?"

"No. How can I? He is a man and he would likely see it as challenging him. But he never brings it up so I remain silent."

"Do you really think he would take it as disrespect?"

"Most men here would."

Joanna thought for a moment before responding, "I suppose you are right."

"And when I shared a little of my concern with Mama, she encouraged me to pray over whether God wants me to marry Matthew or not. I have been praying for a week with no answer."

Joanna smiled lovingly, "You know sometimes God tells us to wait."

"I know." I smiled and started to laugh. "But I want to know now," I said in a whiney voice. Joanna and I both laughed hard.

Once we regained some composure, Joanna said, "You have about a year and a half. I am quite confident God will show you by then."

I smiled. "Thank you, Joanna."

Silence fell again. I drank some hot cocoa, which was now warm cocoa. I was searching for the best approach to talk about visiting the city and decided to just be direct.

"Did Josiah talk to you about the opportunity of visiting the city this summer?"

"Yes. He told me he and you had been invited to join Samuel and Amelia," she answered almost flatly.

This tone always bothered me. It was the one time I could not read between the lines. "And?" I questioned.

It was her turn to tear up. "I am not sure how I feel about it. I suppose part of me is jealous. I do not want to leave the town but knowing I will never be allowed to leave and my betrothed is, I almost want to go with him. Part of me wants to beg him to stay. But if he wants to go, I love and trust him enough to follow this opportunity, wherever it leads."

I smiled at her. "God has truly led you. I am so blessed to have a friend like you."

She smiled back. "Have you decided?"

"Yes. I am going, surprisingly, with Matthew's blessing." Joanna's smile changed slightly but she kept her thoughts to herself. "It has caused me to think that he may have doubts about our engagement as well. Perhaps that is God's answer."

"Maybe," she replied then looked at me sharply. "You are not considering leaving for good, are you? The way your uncle did?"

"I do not know, Joanna. Perhaps. Right now I am unsure of what I want for the future. The thought has recently crossed my mind."

"Sarai, you cannot!" Joanna almost yelled at me. "If you leave, I will never get to see or talk to you again. You are my best friend and future sister-in-law. We have waited our whole lives to be sisters. I do not want to have to shun you."

"You do not have to do that."

"If you leave I will have to make good friends with others so I cannot go against the way of the town."

"Josiah would still write to me." There was a moment of silence. Finally I said, "Forget I mentioned that, Joanna. I am praying about what God wants to do with me. I will go this summer and return, hopefully with some clarity."

She gave me a small smile. "I wish I were as brave as you, Sarai."

"It is not bravery at this point. It is restlessness. It is like I have one hundred horses inside fighting to get out and run free. I have been offered an outlet for it and I want to seize it."

Silence rose again between us and lingered until we both decided we needed to pray over these things. And pray we did.

We decided to eat lunch at my house so Joanna could see Josiah. Mama greeted us as soon as we walked in the door with hugs and the aroma of food. "Did you girls have a good morning together?" she asked, taking our shawls and blankets.

"Yes, Mama," I replied, giving her a kiss on the cheek. The three of us walked over to the table. Mama prayed for us and Joanna and I ate all the food that was left from family lunch. Apparently heavy emotional discussions lead to extreme hunger.

We three chatted lightly as we ate. Josiah came in after a while and smiled at the sight of Joanna. She stood and greeted him and he joined us at the table. We continued talking until Mama got up to start dinner. Joanna decided it was time to head to her house, so Josiah and I bundled up to walk Joanna home.

As we walked, I decided to hold back a couple of feet so they could talk about the summer. Joanna openly shared her feelings and reservations but said she would be all right if he went. He smiled at her and I was reminded of why we had chaperones.

We bid Joanna good night and started the walk back to our house. Once we were down the road a ways, I asked, "What do you think, Josiah?"

He started, as if I had broken his train of thought. "What do I think about what?"

"Going to the city," I replied, trying not to sound annoyed.

"Oh, that," he said trying to sound like he had not already been thinking about it. "I am still unsure, Sarai. I am not sure either one of us should go."

"Why is that?"

"It is our family history that causes my doubt. What if we go and end up finding out we want to live out there instead of here?"

"What if we do?"

Josiah's eyes grew wide and he stopped dead in his tracks while turning to look at me, "I cannot do that to Joanna. I love her too much."

I looked Josiah square in the eyes and asked, "Then why are you so worried?"

He broke gaze, looking down at the ground. "I do not know."

"If you love her, truly love her and she truly trusts you, as I know she does, and you know this is where you are meant to be, where is the harm in taking a short vacation for a once-in-a-lifetime opportunity? Do not let fear make your decision."

Josiah looked back at me and smiled. "When did you become so wise?"

"I do not know if wise is the best word, but I am going and it would be nice to have you along. I know Samuel would really like having you there."

"You are right, Sarai." Josiah turned and started walking again.

We walked in silence for several yards before Josiah inquired, "What did Matthew say?"

I smiled to myself as I said, "He told me to go."

Josiah stopped dead again. "He did!" he exclaimed in disbelief. "Just like that, without question or reservation?"

I chuckled. "It surprised me as well, but I am so thankful because I had already decided I was going no matter what he said."

"You would go even if he disapproved?"

"Yes. He is not my husband yet, so he does not have authority over me. I believe God is telling me to go, and if God told me to do something, I would go against Matthew even if we were married."

Josiah's jaw dropped. "You have given this a lot of thought, Sarai. Are you planning to leave permanently?"

"I am not planning anything, but if God told me to live in the city, I would do it, in spite of the consequences that may come, since I know Papa and Mama would support me."

Josiah stared at me for a few moments as what I had said sunk into his mind. "You are serious," he stated with a look of genuine concern.

"I am, Josiah. If God clearly told you to go, would you not leave your homeland?"

"I do not know if I could."

"Then maybe God is wanting you to go this summer to know that you can leave even though you know you belong here with Joanna."

"Perhaps."

"I am going, Josiah. I believe God is going to teach me something this summer. I need to go."

"I should go to keep an eye on you." We both laughed and started walking again. "I will pray over it tonight, and in the morning, so we can tell them after dinner tomorrow.

"That sounds like a good idea, since they are leaving the next morning," I said. We walked mostly in silence but the excitement began to well inside me again. I wanted to run and sing, but I forced myself to stay calm by my brother's side until we reached our house.

*****

Dinner the next evening seemed to last forever. Josiah would not give any indication of his decision no matter how hard or sweetly I looked at him. It continued into family devotional until all of the other children were in bed and Josiah and I were told to come back downstairs. We sat in the living area with Samuel, Amelia, Papa, and Mama.

Samuel said, "Tonight is decision time. What say you?" He looked at Josiah first.

Josiah looked back and said slowly, "I have decided to go."

I jumped up and gave him a hug squealing. "Me too!" Mama shushed me since the other children were in bed. "I am sorry," I said with a small giggle, putting my hand over my mouth.

"I am so glad," Samuel said with a huge smile. "We will have a great summer together."

Papa then said cautiously, "I do not want you bragging about this. It will be challenging enough without extra emotion. Your

33

mother and I will talk with the other children when the time gets closer."

"Yes, sir," Josiah and I said in unison.

"Off to bed now," Papa said, nodding toward the stairs. We gave hugs all around and kissed Mama before heading to bed.

I was not sleepy and listened to the hushed voices downstairs though I could not make out what was said. All I could think was, "I am going to the city!"

CHAPTER 7

Winter turned into spring. We prepared the land for planting. The April showers came to nourish the ground. Life went on as usual, and my excitement grew each day. It was difficult hiding it at school and not discussing it with Joanna in public places, but somehow I managed to stay calm and focus on my lessons during the day and let my imagination wander during the evenings. I tried so hard to imagine what it would look like from what Samuel had shared, but it was completely inadequate.

Samuel and Amelia came home the first week of May. That evening during family devotional, Papa explained the summer to all of the kids. The little ones found the news exciting and the middle ones wanted to know why they were not allowed to come with us. Papa handled it brilliantly, as usual, and everyone seemed satisfied.

The next week seemed to crawl and fly at the same time. Once I finished my school lessons, I felt so free. I allowed my excitement to show at home and it was wonderful, though challenging not to overdo it.

The afternoon before we were to leave, we had a small gathering at our home with the March family, the Safford family, and some of the extended family who did not think that Papa and Mama were making a huge mistake.

It was beautiful outside. The flowers were blooming and the trees were plump with green. The sky was bright blue with wisps of cloud scattered here and there. The men moved tables and chairs to the porch and side yard while the women put the food on the serving area in the kitchen. Papa blessed the food and the chaos of getting food for all commenced. The "kids" all gathered at the tables in the side yard; the girls at one and the boys at the other. We all ate hungrily and chatted lightly. When the middle and younger children finished eating, they all went to play.

We older girls huddled at one end to talk. We talked about the family and my cousins whose babies were due soon. There fell a moment of silence, which rarely happens, so Rivka, my cousin, looked around then said, "You know, Sarai, you are so fortunate." She looked at me with a sweet smile. "Ever since Uncle Mark left, if the word vacation comes out of one of our mouths, Papa goes into a rant. Even Mama is paranoid. When they heard Uncle John was allowing you to go to the city I thought Papa was going to explode."

"Mine as well," interjected Camilla, another cousin. "I think my Papa feels a little responsible, being the oldest in the family."

"But why are they so worried about it?" inquired Saphira, the third of the pregnant cousins. "Just because one person left does not mean the other one hundred of us will."

"None of us knows what it did to them when he left," Camilla responded. "We can speculate, but it is never discussed. All we see is anger when we mention wanting to see outside."

"This is true," Saphira said and we nodded in agreement.

"Well, maybe once you all return, they will realize a visit to the city is only a visit and not a sign someone will leave," Rivka offered. "I would love to see the beach just one time."

And so those who could not leave discussed what they would like to see out there.

A little while later, Papa called the adults and teenagers into the living room while the little ones stayed outside and played. He asked Samuel, Amelia, Josiah, and me to the middle of the group. "As you know, my children are going away for the summer to visit the city. I am thankful for you who support my wife and me as we send them for this educational experience." At that moment, my eyes met Matthew's and I thought I saw a hint of a tear. I quickly looked away and back at Papa. "As we send them we ask for prayer for them, for us, and for the Safford family as their daughter goes with her husband." All nodded. "I would like to have a time of prayer now, especially for what our children will learn from the outside world." Almost every person in that room prayed for us. It was amazing! It also helped greatly to know that we were not alone in this.

Sleep would not come to me that night as I tossed and turned in my bed. Reflecting on the prayer time that evening, I realized how many people truly cared and wanted the best for my brothers and me. When it was time to go home, Joanna did not want to let Amelia and me go. We all cried a little as we thought about the separation. Amelia and I would be each other's strength but Joanna would really be alone.

Papa and Mama allowed all of us to sleep a bit later the next morning, but when I smelled Mama's cooking, I put on my robe and went down to the kitchen. Mama was just putting some bread on the fire and Papa was making coffee, so neither of them heard me approach. Mama jumped when she saw me.

"Sarai! What are you doing awake?" she asked with surprise on her face. "We wanted all of you to get some extra rest."

I glowed at her with big eyes. "I was awake most of the night. The excitement and anticipation as well as thoughts of the beautiful party kept my mind going, but I am not at all tired."

"Are you ready for today?" Mama asked with a smile.

"Yes, ma'am. I need to check my bags, but I believe most everything is ready to go."

"I am proud of you for trying the city, Sarai," Papa said boldly. "It will be a great time of learning for you."

"Thank you, Papa." I gave him a big hug and he gave a big squeeze back.

Feet began to hit the floor upstairs and my brothers and sisters came down stairs. The little ones played on the rug in the family room. The rest of us gathered around the table and sipped our cups of coffee while Mama continued breakfast. As she placed the food on the table, there came a knock at the door. Miriam ran to answer it.

"Samuel!" she exclaimed, opening the door wide. He picked up Miriam and carried her to the table, Amelia following right behind them.

"Right on time," Mama said, giving Samuel and Amelia each a hug. We all moved to our places at the table and Papa prayed over the food and for safe travel to the city for us. I ate quickly and asked to be excused so I could get ready to go. I put my dishes away and ran upstairs to get dressed and check my bags.

All of my summer clothes were in my duffel bag. In my purse my hair brush, journal, extra paper, some of my Shakespeare plays and my Bible. I grabbed a pen and some ink and placed them carefully in my bag. I was ready.

Taking my things down to the entry way, I set them by the door and went to help clean up the kitchen. Once everything was cleaned, Papa gathered everyone in the living room to pray. Each person prayed, and Papa closed the prayer time. Next came all the hugs and tears. As Mama hugged me, she said, "I love you. Listen to God's voice and learn as much as you can."

I started to tear up. "I will. I love you, Mama."

We collected our bags and headed to the wagon where Papa was hitching up the horses. The boys loaded the luggage and helped Amelia and me into the buggy. They followed, and Papa jumped in the front. He signaled the horses and we were on our way.

They all waved at us and we waved back. Slowly, they faded into the distance. We rode through town and saw many disapproving looks as we passed. Knowing how much my neighbors disagreed gave me a spark of energy and I had to hide a smirk. *They are jealous*, I thought.

We rode to the next town and unloaded at the bus station. I expected to get on the bus until Samuel motioned us to the parking lot. There was a car there that was for us. He opened the trunk and he put our bags inside. I hugged Papa and he kissed my forehead. "I love you, Papa."

"I love you, Sarai. Have a great time," he said, smiling at me. He hugged my brothers and we loaded in the car. "Drive safely."

Samuel cranked the engine and we were on our way.

CHAPTER 8

The car was silent for quite some time. I had never been in a car before, and I stared out of the window as the world flew by us. It was scenery I was used to, but to see it whirl by in a blur was fascinating. Fascinating, until I started to feel nauseous. I had to put my head back and closed my eyes for a minute.

Samuel must have noticed because he broke my thoughts saying, "Are you feeling all right, Sarai?"

The break in silence startled me. "What? Oh, yes, Samuel, I am fine, thank you. I was getting a little nauseated from the trees whirling by the window."

"It does take some getting used to, riding in a car." Samuel laughed.

Amelia laughed as well and said, "Indeed. My first trip in the car I vomited from the motion."

"Really?" I asked laughing as well. "Perhaps we should keep talking. It seems to be helping my stomach."

"I agree," Amelia said. "And if you need it, I have some medicine that helps to settle the stomach."

"That is good to know."

We continued to chat and I started asking questions about the city to which we were going. I received a lot of cryptic answers as Samuel clearly wanted to surprise us with how it would be. After talking about half an hour, I realized Josiah had said nothing since we left the station. He was simply looking out the window.

"Josiah," I said, touching his arm. He started. "Are you all right?"

He blinked and shook his head before replying, "Yes. I am fine."

"You look as if you are deep in thought," Samuel said.

"I am," said Josiah. "I am thinking about what this will really be like and wondering if I have made a mistake."

No one responded and silence lingered in the car for quite some time. Then I saw the first tall building and broke the silence, "That is the biggest building I have ever seen!"

Samuel laughed nervously and said, "Just you wait. There are things here you cannot imagine. I have so many surprises."

"What kind of surprises?" Josiah almost yelled.

Samuel became a little hot at this exclamation, "Now do not be like that, Josiah. I am not going to spoil the fun, and if you are going to sulk the whole vacation, I will send you home."

Josiah said nothing and stared out the window again. I had never seen him this way before, and it was beginning to frighten me. I kept silent, however, and went back to taking in the sights.

I started to see taller and larger buildings. The tree numbers diminished and the number of buildings increased. So this was a city. While the largest buildings were still a bit ahead of us, Samuel pulled off the interstate and drove down suburb streets. We soon turned onto a street with houses, lots of houses. I could not believe how many houses and how close together they stood. Where did people grow their food? Where did their children play? Everything looked so artificial and cramped. It was quite strange.

After passing what felt like a hundred houses and turning down several roads, we pulled into a driveway in front of a spectacularly large home. *Where are we?* I thought, not daring to begin a potential argument. Then a realization of where we might be dawned on me and in moments my suspicions were confirmed. A man who resembled Papa, a woman, and five children (one who could have been my twin with shoulder length hair) came out of the house. They looked like us and yet quite different, especially with the females wearing short pants. I stared in shock. The family I grew up thinking I would never see was now standing directly in front of me. Words cannot express the thoughts and emotions that were flooding my mind.

Samuel greeted my uncle while Amelia greeted the rest. Samuel turned to Josiah and me, waved his arm, and said, "Come here, you two. I want to introduce you to some wonderful people. This is our family: Uncle Mark, Aunt Dianna, Evalynn, Denise, Gail, Jonathan, and Claire." He pointed to each of them as he said their names, then walked over to us and said, "This is my brother, Josiah, and my sister, Sarai," pushing us toward them.

Uncle Mark came forward, shook Josiah's hand and said, "Welcome to our home! We are so glad you are here." He spoke almost identically to Papa. The rest of the family smiled and nodded. "Jonathan, help me get the bags. Please go inside and make yourself at home."

Evalynn (the one who could be my twin) came to me and pulled me in the house. I clutched my purse and allowed her to drag me as fast as she could. Fear started to pour over me. I was so sure of this just five minutes before, but now I wondered if I was ready for this.

The house was enormous! Evalynn took me down a flight of stairs saying, "It is so nice to meet you, Sarai. I have wondered about you, all of you, for a long time. It's so weird having family you don't know." At the bottom of the stairs, she pointed to a room and said, "You will be staying with me. I hope that's okay."

I stared for a few seconds before walking into the room. There were two twin beds, a dresser, a desk, and a closet. The room was the same size as the room my sisters and I shared at home. "Which bed do you want?" Evalynn asked, interrupting my thoughts.

I turned and looked at my mirror image. This is when the fear ended and excitement flooded in me once again. "Oh, Evalynn!" I exclaimed hugging her. "I am so excited to be here. Papa has told us about all of you. I have prayed for years that we would meet. It is like a dream. Oh, I apologize, you asked which bed I would like. It does not matter to me. I am simply thankful to be here."

Evalynn smiled. "Just choose one. This is your home, too."

"I will sleep on the right then." I walked over and put my purse down. Jonathan came a minute later with my duffle and sat it on the bed.

41

"Come on," Evalynn said, pulling me upstairs again. "Mom made lunch for you guys and I'm starving."

We went to their dining room with a large table but not as big as the one at home. Uncle Mark blessed the meal and we passed the food around the table.

Uncle Mark began to ask questions of recent happenings in our town. We gave him a brief overview from the last few months including all the new babies and how all of his family was doing. Once he was satisfied questions came from the cousins. They wanted to know what it was like for Josiah and me, but I ended up answering the majority of the questions. Josiah stared blankly, picked at his food, and only answered when directly spoken to. I was waiting for an explosion similar to the car ride, but it did not come. The rest of us ate while conversing. Aunt Dianna told us the plans for the week, including church and the opportunity to go to school with Evalynn. This was exciting to me and I could not wait to see church and school in the city.

CHAPTER 9

"Sarai, it's eight," Evalynn said, shaking my shoulder lightly. "We need to get ready for church."

I opened my eyes to see the sun peeking through the window. "It is eight o'clock already. I usually awaken before the sun." I quickly got out of bed and began to get ready.

"No need to rush. We have a little time," Evalynn said with a smile. I slowed my pace slightly, but hunger urged me to hurry. As I began to head upstairs in my church clothes, Evalynn stopped me. "Aren't you going to take a shower?"

I turned and looked at her with confusion. "I am sorry? What is a shower?"

"You know, washing your body," she said with a similar expression.

"You mean a bath. No, I will take one this evening," and I turned to go to the kitchen. Amelia was finishing breakfast when I entered. "Good morning, Amelia."

"Good morning, Sarai," she responded with a smile.

"Why did you not wake me? I would have helped you prepare breakfast."

"I wanted you to have some rest. This is your first vacation."

"And most likely my only one. Thank you, Amelia, but I will not let you do it all on your own the entire time."

"We can argue about it later," Amelia said with a wink.

I waited for a few minutes, but only Evalynn came up to join us. "You can go ahead and eat," she said. "It'll be awhile 'til the rest of the family comes."

"You do not eat breakfast together?" I questioned.

"If Amelia wasn't here, we'd be eating cereal or frozen waffles. We like having her homemade breakfast every morning." Evalynn grinned at Amelia who smiled with a little bow.

Clearly, the city was quite different from home and I had a lot to learn.

*****

As we approached the church, my mouth gaped. I could not believe it was a church. It had a steeple, but the rest looked like a large building. Evalynn took my hand, dragging me to the youth building with a "See ya later" to her parents over her shoulder. "You're gonna love this, Sarai! Everyone is so excited to meet you!" We entered the building and heads turned to look at us. People stopped talking to stare. My modest skirt and blouse with scarf were quite the contrast to the jeans and shirts of most of the other teens. This lasted about thirty seconds until a girl ran at us and hugged Evalynn.

"Hey, girl! Who's your twin?" the girl said excitedly.

"This is my cousin Sarai that I told you about."

"It's great to finally meet you! I'm Amberly," she said, extending her hand. "Sam has told us some about you."

"He has?" I questioned, shaking Amberly's hand.

"Amberly spends a lot of time at our house," Evalynn interjected. "We have been friends most of our lives, so she has met Samuel and Amelia. They told anyone who would listen that you were coming."

I felt my face flush. "Really?" I said quietly.

"Of course!" Evalynn exclaimed. "Why wouldn't they? Amelia was ecstatic that you would be coming to help keep her company and y'all could both keep each other from getting homesick."

I smiled to myself wondering if I would become homesick. "I love Amelia and I am so thankful to be here with her."

More people trickled into the building as we talked. I continually met people and knew there was no way I could remember all of the names. I just smiled and nodded with a short "Nice to meet you." After a while music began to play and I was shuffled with a group of girls to a big room with a stage. A band played loudly, but it was clearly meant to draw everyone to worship. I stood in front of a chair and stared at a wall with words that I could understand but did not recognize. Some people were clapping, others standing stiff as I and still others talked, paying no attention to what was happening. *This is church?* I thought.

"Well, not exactly," Evalynn answered. Apparently I had spoken my thought. "This is the youth time. We sing and have announcements and then go to Sunday school before church."

I simply nodded at her as I did not understand what she was talking about but knew you should not talk during church or whatever they called it.

A second song began to play. That is when he walked into the room: tall and extremely handsome. It was difficult not to stare. His twinkling hazel eyes met mine and he smiled with a nod. I quickly looked back at the words on the wall and reminded myself I was there to focus on God.

The song finished and a middle-aged man got on the stage to share announcements and pray. When he dismissed us, Evalynn took my hand and dragged me to another room. Here several girls our age gathered and a young woman who looked just twenty.

The moment the young woman spotted us, she came over and asked, "Evalynn, is this who I think it is?"

Evalynn grinned. "Yup! This is my cousin Sarai."

The woman stuck out her hand to shake mine. "I'm so glad to finally meet you. I'm Kara Leland, the teacher of this class."

"It is nice to meet you as well, Mrs. Leland," I replied with a smile as we shook hands.

"Please call me Kara."

"I am sorry? I do not understand. You said you are a teacher, did you not?"

"Yes."

"As a teacher and authority over us, you deserve respect."

"You are sweet, but it's fine to call me Kara."

I nodded but said nothing more. Evalynn introduced me to the others. A couple were friendly, others gave me odd looks. There was a combination of frivolous talk and Scripture. I was amazed that we were even allowed to talk and ask questions, though I decided not to that day. Mrs. Leland seemed to genuinely care but only three of the girls did.

A bell rang. Mrs. Leland closed in prayer and I left on Evalynn's arm as she took me back out to the sanctuary. It filled with people sitting on benches. A man with a guitar and a woman at a piano began to play and sing. Some clapped, some swayed, some crossed their arms. This was far different than standing with arms by your side as still as a stone statue except for your lips singing the words. I was unsure what I thought of this. I listened to the words of the songs. They were pretty and celebrated God. We sang one hymn I knew, and so I sang with it.

As the pastor preached, I could feel something different. There was life in his words. He really spoke of Jesus and what life in Him meant. This excited me. I knew I would learn a lot from him this summer and really learn about Jesus.

After the service, the youth gathered to talk about where people would be going to lunch. That was when I saw him again. I stared as he asked, "Evalynn, who's your friend?"

"This is Sarai, my cousin. Surely you have heard me mention her. She is staying with us for the summer."

"Really?" he said with interest. I felt myself flush a little. "I'm Austin," he said sticking out his hand.

I looked at his hand then slowly back to his eyes. "It is nice to meet you." I replied, not extending my own hand but looking back down at his.

"It's a handshake."

I looked quickly back at his eye. "I am aware of this greeting, but I cannot share it with you," my tone slightly angrier than I intended.

He looked completely confused. "What? Why not?"

"Because you are a boy."

"What does that have to do with anything?"

"I may only have purposeful physical contact with males who are relatives. You are not a relative, so I cannot shake your hand."

I must have looked angry for he jumped back saying, "Sorry! How am I supposed to know that? Here boys and girls shake hands all the time. They even hug!" He put his arm around Evalynn.

"They do?" I knew I had all kinds of questions on my face.

"Is this boy bothering you, Sarai?" I jumped at the sound of my brother's voice.

"No, Josiah," I said looking at him. "We were only talking."

"Hi. I'm Austin." He extended his hand to Josiah.

Josiah shook it firmly. "Josiah. Sarai is my sister and she is betrothed, so your interest needs to be placed elsewhere." Josiah looked stern.

"I was just saying hello, man. That's all." Austin looked scared. I flushed again.

"We need to go, Sarai." He put his hands around my shoulders and we walked away. We walked past our family. Josiah stopped in front of Samuel. "This was a mistake." I just looked at the ground. He nudged me on and we went to the car.

CHAPTER 10

I was thankful Josiah waited until we returned to the house to talk to me. Lunch had been tense, but he had managed self-control. Aunt Dianna must have told the kids to go to their rooms as they went immediately with little noise. I attempted to go downstairs but was quickly stopped by a hand on my shoulder.

I turned to find Josiah standing over me. "We have not been here twenty-four hours and you have already begun to play the harlot!"

"That is not what I was doing, Josiah," I said softly, looking into his fierce blue eyes.

"You were talking socially with a man more than you ought. What would you call it?"

"I was explaining to him why I could not shake his hand."

Uncle Mark spoke up, "I watched the whole thing, Josiah. She did nothing." This was a mistake.

"I see how well you train your children!" Josiah yelled turning to Uncle Mark. "You watched as that man put his hands on your daughter and did nothing. You have no respect for God, no propriety. You care nothing for your family or your upbringing. You shamed all of us and we are carrying your burden until this day. I thought coming here would help me understand, but I was wrong. How could you exchange good for such evil?"

Uncle Mark stayed calm as he answered, "I realized too late I had made a mistake. When I attempted to return, I had already been shunned. There was nothing to be done to change it."

"I do not believe you!" Josiah yelled. "You love this world more than your family, your town, and our traditions. We know how people should live and you rejected us!"

Uncle Mark said nothing, but the hurt welled in his eyes.

Josiah continued, "It was clearly a mistake to come here and be around such indecency. Sarai and I shall leave tomorrow."

I started at the sound of my name. "I do not wish to go," I said.

"Have you so quickly forgotten that I am your elder and that you will do as I say?" This cut deep. Josiah and I had always been close being Irish twins and he had never pulled rank on me.

Thankfully Samuel came to the rescue. "Josiah, have *you* so quickly forgotten that *I* am the eldest and that you *both* are in *my* charge?" Josiah turned with a glare. "If Sarai wishes to stay, she may."

"You are siding with him?" Josiah pointed at Uncle Mark in disgust.

"I am doing as Papa and Mama requested. They wanted both of you to experience another way of life, to see more of the world."

"They cannot know what it is like here. When I tell them, they will send for Sarai straight away. Mark my words!"

"We shall see. As for leaving, it will be at least a week. We must send a letter to be sure they can collect you in town, as you must take a bus back."

"I must wait a week? What will I do? I want no part of this place."

"So be it. Stay in your room, and I will tell you when you may go home."

Josiah looked as if he wanted to say more, but instead he turned and stormed off to his room.

There was a moment where no one even dared to breathe. When it was clear he was not coming back down, I went to my eldest brother. "Thank you, Samuel," I said softly.

He smiled tenderly. "I had a notion something might occur, but this was not what I had expected. And if you had done something wrong, I would have gotten to you first." He grinned widely. "If you decide to shake hands, know that I will not interfere." I smiled but was shocked. Samuel turned to Uncle Mark. "I wish I could apologize for my brother's actions. I will try to talk with him after supper, but I do not think he will budge. I will send my parents a letter tomorrow."

*****

Back in Evalynn's room, I sat at the desk and wrote in my journal. I had planned to write letters to Joanna and Matthew but now I was at a loss as to what to say to them. I told my journal all and begin to cry as I thought of Josiah's reaction and treatment of Uncle Mark. I would never have imagined my brother and friend could treat anyone that way and yet there it was.

What has happened to my brother, my friend? Why would he treat Uncle Mark with so much disrespect. He spoke of our traditions and yet he broke them because of his anger. I am extremely happy to be here, but is it worth it to lose my brother? Yes, I know I am to be here. I know God has a plan and purpose for me here. I hope Josiah changes his mind and decides to stay. But if not, that must be God's plan for him.

Josiah did not join us for supper. Aunt Dianna did her best to make conversation normal, though the tension from lunch had greatly increased. She told us about the summer activities that would be happening; many of them church youth activities. It was overwhelming hearing it all. I did not know there were so many things to do in this world. I looked forward to many new adventures.

CHAPTER 11

We awoke at 6:30 a.m. to get ready for school. Though Josiah's tantrum was still weighing on me, I dressed quickly and kept a smile on my face. I would not allow his closed mindedness to affect my vacation. Amelia and Aunt Dianna had made a beautiful home like breakfast already and I devoured it. In the midst of all of the others scrambling to get ready, Samuel quietly informed me that Josiah would be leaving next Tuesday as long as Papa could collect him then. It saddened my heart a little more, but I knew if Samuel could not persuade him, no one could.

We arrived at the high school and I could not believe my eyes. It was easily ten times the size of our modest school house and was only for the upper grades. A loud noise alerted us to go to our first class, British Literature. I sat behind Evalynn who was explaining what we would be doing when someone sat in the desk next to me. I took no notice until I heard, "Hey, Sarai!" with a hand next to my desk.

I started and looked to see Austin's huge grin. "Good morning, Austin," I said, looking down at his hand.

"Oh right," he said, and jerked his hand back. "Sorry, I forgot. You didn't tell me you were coming to school."

"I do not recall you asking me." The words escaped my mouth before I checked them or my tone. At home it would have been unthinkable to speak to a boy that way. I considered apologizing, but the teacher began the class before I could take any action.

I tried desperately to pay attention as literature is my favorite subject, but my mind was all over the place. Not only was Josiah in my head, now this boy was there too. Something about him had my attention, and I did not know if it was good.

*****

When lunchtime arrived, he was right there again. I sat with Evalynn and Amberly and soon Austin was in the seat next to me. My heart raced and I tried to only look at my food.

"Have I done something to offend you?" he asked abruptly.

I pondered this question as I continued to stare at my food. The answer came quickly. "I am unsure. I am not used to this behavior, and I honestly do not know how to handle it."

"I'm just trying to help you feel welcomed, but if you want me to leave you alone, just say so."

I finally looked at him but said nothing. My head was spinning, attempting to process the information. Was that all he was doing? Helping me to feel welcome? If that was the case, then why did none of the other boys talk to me except in passing? They were friendly but not like this. I could not comprehend. I was not sure how much my confusion showed as I looked into his eyes, but I never responded as Evalynn broke my thoughts and gaze to introduce me to another friend.

*****

For the remainder of the day, I was unable to concentrate on anything said in the classrooms. I was thankful that I would not be tested on any of the material so my mind could wander. I tried to pray but I kept thinking of what I was feeling in my heart and trying to figure out what Austin was thinking. Could I just be friends with a boy?

*****

When we arrived home from school, Aunt Dianna had a snack for us and asked about the day. She was curious about the differences and I explained. When we finished our conversation, she handed me a letter from home. I was surprised to receive a letter so quickly. I ran to my room and tore open the letter. I was even more surprised to discover it was from Matthew. I sat on the bed and read:

My darling Sarai,

 I pray that your family and you had a safe trip to the city. I am quite certain that even in a couple of days you have already seen much. I know this is a bit unorthodox but I wanted to tell you to enjoy every moment. I want you to experience as much of the culture as you can. This is a rare opportunity and I want you to take advantage of it, no matter what it brings. I love you, Sarai, and I look forward to hearing about your adventures. May God bless your time in the city.

Your beloved,
Matthew

My eyes welled with tears. Except for the night of our discussion about the summer, he had never spoken to me that way. It was difficult to fully understand if he was releasing me because of the wording, but I decided to stop thinking about the situation so much and to simply enjoy the adventures, come what may.

After dinner as I was preparing for bed, I asked Evalynn if I might borrow some clothes. As part of experiencing the culture, I decided to try dressing like they did. She led me to her closet and chest of drawers that were both full of clothing. I was a bit overwhelmed at the number of choices. I was not quite ready to wear pants yet so I found a beautiful floral-print skirt and a light-green polo shirt to wear the next day. I smiled as I went to sleep and dreamed of what the rest of the week would hold.

CHAPTER 12

The next morning, I was ready to face the day. My body woke me up around 5:00 a.m., which is more normal for me. I brushed my hair, donned my "modern" clothes, and went to the kitchen where Aunt Dianna was helping Amelia with breakfast. I went to help and learned how to boil water on an electric stove. The others trickled in for breakfast around 6:45 a.m. The female cousins gushed at my outfit telling me I looked "super cute." I smiled and kept eating. It was odd getting compliments when you were not used to them.

When we arrived at school, a few of the girls who knew me were astonished at my "new look." Many compliments came and I was asked to take a spin. I felt awkward being fussed over, but it was nice to be praised for looking nice.

The bell rang and we headed for literature class. As we entered the hallway, I spotted Austin coming from the other end. He saw us. As our eyes met, he stopped dead in his tracks and his jaw dropped. Oh to know what he was thinking! I felt the heat rise toward my face and quickly looked away. Austin's feet began moving toward us slowly and stopped in front of us just outside of the classroom door.

"Sarai." Austin looked me up and down. I had to look at the ground. "You look beautiful."

Even more blood rushed to my face. "Thank you," I said, still looking at the ground. The warning bell rang and I stepped around Austin to go into class. Evalynn and Austin came in on my heels.

I could see Austin trying not to look at me out of the corner of my eye. I tried not to notice him looking. I felt flattered but awkward all at the same time. This was a new feeling I could not place, but I decided it was part of the experience.

The entire day was like that. Everyone who knew me gave me a compliment and even a few that did not know me. The blushing slowed down with each compliment until I simply felt beautiful. I thought, *I could get used to this. If only Matthew would look at me this way.*

*****

Later that afternoon, I asked Evalynn, "Are compliments always given so freely here?"

"It depends on the person, but yeah," she responded

"How nice it is," I trailed off in thought of home. There was such an emphasis on denying self and avoiding vanity to keep ourselves "righteous" and pure. We all dressed mostly the same as to avoid any one standing out at all. I decided then that though it was against my culture I would tell those I loved how beautiful and wonderful they were. I started with Evalynn. "Evalynn, you are a beautiful young woman. Thank you for welcoming me so readily."

She turned to me stunned. "You're welcome," she said with a slight tone of question.

"I am practicing compliments."

"Good start. We'll work on it."

"Thank you." Evalynn turned to her studies and I went to my journal.

Because of his silence and lack of appearance, I had almost forgotten Josiah was still in the house until we returned home from school on Thursday. As we entered the house, my brothers' raised voices barreled down the stairs. Though unexpected and disturbing, it became worse as I realized they were fighting about me.

"How can you let her out of the house dressed like that!" Josiah demanded.

"I do not understand your problem, Josiah. She is modestly clothed. The style is different, that is all," Samuel attempted to reason with him.

"Those skirts are far too short, the shirts barely have sleeves, and her hair is down for all to see. That is *not* modest."

"She is covered! And why do you care if her hair is down?"

"It is showing off her hair, like a harlot!"

"It is simply different. Do not be so dramatic. You clearly need to see what other city people wear."

"If it is less than that, I do not wish to see it. I will stay in here until I can return home."

Samuel said nothing more. I heard a door close and quickly turned to the counter between the kitchen and living area pretending I had not heard the argument. Amelia gave me a weak smile, and Aunt Dianna attempted to ask about our day with no response. Samuel walked up, sat next to me, and sighed heavily.

"I am sorry you heard that, Sarai," he said with a slight catch in his voice. Amelia came around and put her hands on his shoulders. "I do not know what has happened to him. I do not know this Josiah."

I tried to force a cheerful smile but could not make any of my muscles move except to say, "Thank you for defending me."

Samuel reached over and squeezed my hand. I had always been closer to Josiah but currently they were trading places. The silence loomed. Aunt Dianna put a plate of cookies on the counter but no one ate them.

When I finally gathered the will to move, I picked up my bag and went to my room. Pulling out my journal and ink, I sat at the desk and began to write. Four lines in the tears pushed their way out of my eyes. I tried to stop them but it was futile. The flow came harder until I was sobbing, hands covering my face. I do not know how long I had been crying when arms embraced me. I did not look up to see who it was, I simply gave in, falling into their shirt crying that much harder.

It felt like hours before I was able to regain control and when I finally looked up, Aunt Dianna was smiling back at me. "How do you live like this?" I asked through shortened breath.

Aunt Dianna's smile grew. "We just do."

I began to think I should just return home. Better never to have come to the city than to have your whole family turn their backs on you. "Maybe I should go home."

There was no surprise on her face. She simply said, "Is that what you want to do?"

"No, but it has to be better than my brother hating me for the rest of our lives. We have always been close friends, and I do not like having him angry with me."

"Sometimes we must do things that others don't like," Aunt Dianna said with a smile. "It is part of growing up. They can be for right or wrong reasons, but I think yours are good, so I think you should stay. I think your parents want you to stay, too. And Evalynn has been looking forward to this summer for almost a year."

"I think you are right. I will stay and learn from this."

She smiled and gave me a big hug. I turned back to my journal and was left in silence.

*****

At breakfast Saturday morning, I found out it was a fun day. I was to learn about the great women's favorite pastime of shopping. Evalynn whispered to me that it was a way to get me out of the house and not be stuck with Josiah all day. I smiled and nodded in gratitude.

We got dressed and all of the girls piled into the van with no room to spare. We went to a local mall that nearly took my breath away. I had never seen anything so massive. Inside there were shops for everything. I was educated on much.

We went into a store filled with, what I thought to be, under-garments. I learned they were bathing suits and that I would need one for later in the summer. "I cannot wear these," I protested, looking at the lack of material.

"Don't worry," Evalynn reassured me. "There are more in the back that actually cover everything." She took me to the back of the store and showed me some one pieces and tankinis. Our definition of everything was obviously different.

"Evalynn, these do not cover anything."

She pulled a couple of tankinis with shorts and pushed me into a dressing room. "Here, just try these on."

I did as I was told and put on a top with large white flowers and black shorts. It was not bad, but I felt naked in the minimal material that clung to my figure. They assured me I was covered well. To avoid trying on anything else, I said yes to that one and Aunt Diana paid for it.

They graciously allowed me as much time as I wanted in the book store. I could have stayed in there the whole day. There were more books on one shelf than in our whole town! I wanted to buy them all and Aunt Dianna offered to buy me three, all Christian fiction.

We ate lunch in the food court. I had Evalynn choose my food since I had no idea what most things were. A chicken deluxe sandwich and fries is what I ate and, though, much heavier than I was used to, I enjoyed every bite.

After lunch, we finished walking the mall. I know we did not, but it seemed as if we went into every store there. Around dinnertime, we left and picked up pizza on the way home. Until I sat down and melted into the car seat, I had no idea how tired I was. I closed my eyes and let my body give way to the flow of the car.

I must have fallen asleep as the next thing I remember was Evalynn gently shaking my shoulder. "Sarai, we're home."

The pizza was as heavy as lunch and swam in juices. I was only able to eat one piece with a sip of soda. My stomach churned though the flavor was succulent. The family planned to watch a movie so I sat on the sofa next to Evalynn. Still exhausted it took no time for me to return to sleep. So much for my first movie experience.

CHAPTER 13

I do not even remember going to my bed, but I awoke in it at six the next morning feeling refreshed. I debated about what to wear to church but decided to just continue with the city clothes. I then went and helped Amelia with breakfast. As everyone came to the kitchen, the air was still thick, but we were able to converse normally. Josiah refused to go to church. I do not recall him ever skipping church for any reason, not even illness, but there is a first time for everything.

Samuel told me to ride with Amelia and him. Today I did not question and went. The car was silent for just a couple minutes before Samuel spoke. "We need to pray much for Josiah. I plead with him every day to change his mind and stay, but his heart grows harder with every attempt."

I looked down and wrung my hands. I thought for a moment before saying, "Samuel, maybe I could…"

"No, Sarai," Samuel interrupted me. "You are the primary focus of his anger. There is nothing you can do or say to appease him except to say you will leave with him and I will not allow him to push you into leaving since I know you do not wish to leave. The only thing, and the best thing, you can do is pray for God to soften his heart."

I nodded as I caught Samuel's eye in the mirror. Silence stayed until we reached the church.

I did my best to smile. I think people could see something on my face but no one asked. That is until Austin came.

He clearly sought me out and immediately sensed my sadness. He asked, "What's wrong, Sarai?"

I did not know how to answer. I really wanted to cry, but not in the middle of the room and certainly not in front of him. I took a deep breath and said slowly. "My brother, Josiah, is angry with me and he believes this place to be detrimental for us." I held myself together. "He is leaving Tuesday and I cannot talk to him. I may not even be able to say goodbye to him."

"I'm sorry, Sarai," Austin said, touching my shoulder lightly. He forgot the rule and I jumped causing him to remember and move his hand promptly. "Oh, sorry." He squirmed.

I do not know why I responded this way but I said, "It is all right."

We both looked startled and then smiled. My heart was racing and my shoulder tingled from his touch. The music began to play and he motioned for me to walk toward the meeting room. I was thankful for a reason to smile. My mind raced wondering more about these feelings: the heart-racing tingle, the smile, and the excitement. I did not understand these things. I tried to sing, though I still did not know the songs and listened as well as I could with Austin sitting next to me. I was thankful to go to Sunday school with only girls as it helped my concentration. Having gone to the school during the week most of the girls were nicer and said hello at the very least. Thankfully my demeanor had changed and no one noticed that I was still carrying a heavy heart.

Austin decided to sit next to me in church as well. During the greeting time, I allowed him to shake my hand and it was freeing. I felt a small urge to hug him but resisted. That, I thought would be too much but still my heart fluttered with the idea of it.

Service and lunch were a blur. I had already planned to write letters in the afternoon but decided I should journal first, especially since I needed to figure out something before I wrote to Matthew. I told my journal the events of the morning then wrote:

> *What am I feeling? I cannot make sense of this. I do not know what to name it, but my heart is full and it is like it is over flowing. Is it joy? Is it love? He is*

so nice and he is very handsome. I know
with him I would not be trapped. I can be
myself. What a thought!

I sat and contemplated this thought for a while before turning my mind to my letters. I would write to Mama as straight-forwardly as possible, but what to say to Joanna and Matthew I was not sure. Do I warn Joanna about Josiah? Do I tell her about Austin? I cannot tell Matthew about Austin. I wrote Mama first for some practice and then wrote the others about what the city was like, leaving feeling mostly out of it. I decided I would wait until after Josiah returned home and heard what they said before I got into all of that.

It was the last week of their school before the exams. I decided to go instead of sitting at the house all day. When Austin saw me Monday morning, he smiled broadly. I did too. He greeted me with the most tender handshake that lasted longer than it should have, but I let it. Evalynn nudged me and we walked into class. She gave me a questioning look. I smiled slightly and looked down at the ground until I sat in the desk.

Walking to second block, Evalynn said, "What was that?"

I feigned innocence. "I do not know what you mean," I said with a slight smile.

Evalynn laughed. "Don't play games with me. I saw that look between you and Austin."

"I do not know that it was anything."

"Oh, I know something when I see it and that's something. Do you like him?"

"He is a nice and handsome boy. My stomach flutters and my heart races when he is near."

"Then you do like him!" Evalynn exclaimed. "We will so talk about this later. I need the scoop."

I had no idea what she meant, but I nodded as if I did and said nothing more about it.

Austin sat by me at lunch. I talked to all sitting around but he was my primary conversationalist. He asked questions about my home, my family, and me. I asked about his and him. Such different backgrounds and yet we were still similar. We both liked reading and music, though he was not a fan of dancing. We also both liked science. He asked me what I wanted to be when I finished school, but I did not know how to answer as the answer is the same for all women at home. A newly wedded woman would teach in our school until she had her first child, then she would run her home full-time. Austin was considering something in the science realm, like pharmacy.

I thought for a moment, *What would I do if I could choose? I do love literature. Perhaps I would continue to teach. I wonder what other options there are.*

Lunch was so nice but far too short. I began to think about the next time we would talk, what I would share. Honestly, compared to the city my life is pretty dull and uninteresting. But I loved learning about all of the variety here.

*****

Solemnness filled me as I woke up Tuesday morning. Josiah would be leaving while the rest of us were at school. Samuel decided that would be best for all. I pleaded with Samuel to at least try to say goodbye, but Samuel refused. Instead, I wrote him a short letter and asked Samuel to slip it into his bag. Thankfully Samuel did agree to that.

My face was downcast when I arrived at the school. I was already sitting in my English desk when Austin arrived. I did not even look up. He placed a gentle hand on my shoulder and I glanced at him from the corner of my eye, though neither of us said anything.

At lunch he asked how I was doing.

I shook my head. "I am not entirely sure. Mostly I am hurt that my brother and friend is not at all the person I thought he was."

"Well, at least you can have a good time now," he offered.

I was a little taken aback by this. "I suppose that is one way to look at it." I had nothing more to say. I picked at my food and ate to the best of my ability. Austin tried to talk more, but I told him

I did not want to talk just then. He persisted a little but eventually gave up.

Samuel was at the breakfast bar to greet us when we arrived home. He looked as solemn as I felt. Aunt Dianna put snacks on the bar, which we picked at in silence. She made some signal with her head, and my cousins left, Aunt Dianna on their heels. It was only Samuel, Amelia, and I. We all looked at each other for a few moments until the unspoken words killed me.

"Is everything all right?" I blurted.

Samuel sighed deeply. "I really hope they are. Josiah said little but I can tell he is still quite angry, especially since I did not make you leave."

I nodded a silent "thank you."

"We need to pray earnestly that he does not make trouble at home. Since I have never seen him this way, I do not know what he might do."

I nodded in understanding. Samuel grabbed Amelia's and my hands and prayed right then, mostly for protection for our family. At that moment fear gripped me as I tried to imagine what Josiah might do. Would he ruin our family in the town? That could work in my favor but what about the others? It would not be fair to Papa and Mama or my brothers and sisters if they wanted to stay. Surely he would consider what is best for all of them.

*****

As the week went on, the tension waned until Saturday when we finally felt none. Perhaps Austin was right, now I could have fun. I had received a letter from Matthew on Thursday that had been positive. He thanked me for the descriptions of the city and the people. It was odd to hear a sound of hope that he, too, might make it to the city one day with me, but I pretended not to hear it when I wrote my reply. My heart was not his and I knew it, though I knew I had to be careful not to give away my feelings. It was difficult sounding neutral enough to not tell him to go away, but not sound as if I loved him either. I did not want to raise red flags about my feelings and so I had to choose my words carefully.

The next week at the school was for final exams, so I had to stay at the house. It was nice spending some time with Amelia and Aunt Dianna. I learned about being a "suburban housewife" and how things were done on a daily basis. I did not realize how much of the day Samuel and Uncle Mark were gone.

Tuesday, Samuel was home, and I was thankful of that when the mail arrived. There was a letter from Papa and Mama, and I could tell the handwriting was not quite right. Amelia went to get Samuel from their room where he was studying. He came quickly when he heard the news. His hands were shaking slightly as he opened the letter. He read it over, then asked Aunt Dianna to please leave us. When she was upstairs, he had us sit down on the sofa and read the letter aloud to us.

Dear Samuel,

I am not sure who it was you returned to us, but it is not your brother. We expected him to change, but not like this. He is full of anger and hatred and is threatening to tell the whole village where you are. He is also demanding we tell Matthew about the situation. We are very confused and at a loss as to what to do. Please pray that God will grant us much wisdom. We will talk with Matthew so that Josiah will not. Pray that we will explain well and his heart will be soft. Please do not worry and concentrate on your studies. We only wanted to let you know how things are going.

Much love,
Papa and Mama

I had to hide a smile at the thought of Matthew knowing a boy was talking to me. Perhaps it would help him realize that I am not property but a person worthy of love and respect. I also had a heart to be won and not simply given in blind obedience.

*****

Where these thoughts came from, I did not know, but they were empowering. Samuel and Amelia were downcast. I was torn between sadness for what my parents were going through and happiness that Matthew would know about Austin from another source. It was not up to me to "break the news." I did my best to focus on the sadness to be in the same spirit as Samuel and Amelia. Samuel prayed for the situation and then looked at me very seriously.

"I know Matthew will understand," he said grimly, "but you need to be very careful and very certain before you make any decisions." I nodded in understanding trying to look as grim as he. "I have watched Austin and you the last couple of weeks and I see the way you look at each other. I do believe he is a nice boy, but I do not think you will find what you are seeking in him."

I nodded again still trying to look grim. We talked for a few minutes about the implications and complications at home before I was dismissed. I walked as solemnly as I could until I was out of sight then ran to my room and journal. I wrote what happened and what Samuel said, then wrote:

> *I cannot explain how free I feel. It is like a volcano has erupted and I can flow where ever the lava takes me. I can follow my heart toward Austin because, in a sense, Matthew already knows. I do not have to pretend. I will not rub it in his face, I am not cruel, but I can mention things here and there. I can see where this might lead and find out what true love is.*

My hope had been rekindled that it was possible not to get stuck in a marriage but marry my true love. I could marry Austin.

CHAPTER 14

I had not seen Austin all week due to the final examinations. Saturday afternoon, there was an end of the year pool party for the church youth group and I was excited to go. Evalynn helped me with my bathing suit and showed me what to wear over it. She helped calm my nerves about the pool as I did not know how to swim. She asked what I was planning to tell Austin about the letter but I didn't know. Ironically he had not asked about my betrothal after Josiah's public scorn, but I decided not to plan anything and simply see where the conversation went.

My heart raced during the drive. I could not wait to see his handsome face at my first city party. I walked behind Evalynn to the door. She did not bother to knock but walked straight into the house. Mrs. Vaugh, the youth pastor's wife, greeted us, showing us the food and bathrooms if we needed to change. There were a few people there already, but I did not see Austin. Evalynn suggested we go ahead and swim a little before it got too crowded so she could teach me.

The water was colder than I expected. I stopped when the water hit my knees and began to shake. Evalynn had jumped in and was gliding through the water.

"Just jump in and move around," she said.

I was leery of really jumping since I had never done that before, but from the step, I let me body sink into the water up to my chin. I walked around and tried to warm up a little. Evalynn swam over to me and began showing me how to do this and that. It was weird but it seemed like it would end up fun later.

Other people came in, but I was focused on learning how to breathe and swim. I was so focused I jumped out of my skin when I felt some one behind me grab my waist. It was Austin and out of reaction, not thinking, I hit him in the arm, something unthinkable back home.

"Please do not do that. You scared the wits out of me!" I exclaimed.

"Sorry. Just having fun," he said with a grin.

"People do not do such things where I am from, so I do not know that as fun," I said still slightly perturbed.

"Enjoying the water?" he asked

"I suppose. This is my first time swimming so I do not know what I am doing. Evalynn is teaching me." And I turned back to Evalynn. We continued to work on the basics until my stomach was rumbling. We decided to get something to eat and Austin followed.

Once seated, I asked him about his exams and plans for the summer. Evalynn shared about our summer plans. It turned out we were doing a lot of the same things as they were activities with the church. We talked about nothing really. There was no mention from him about my brother or family. He asked more about things I liked and told me how beautiful I looked in my bathing suit. The comment caused me to blush, as I had forgotten my discomfort at the lack of clothing until then.

Austin left to get some sweets, and when he was out of ear shot, Evalynn turned and said, "He is so hitting on you."

"He has not hit me," I replied with a dumbfounded look.

"No, I mean he likes you," Evalynn said laughing.

"How do you know?"

"The way he looks at you and wants to know about you, his compliments. He definitely likes you."

I smiled, blushing. "I think I like him too. I like the way he makes me feel."

Austin walked back to where we sat. He had gotten a cookie and brownie for me and told me I had to decide which I liked better.

Both were quite sweet but the deep chocolate of the brownie really satisfied my taste buds.

"Brownies are my favorite too." He was delighted. "I will get you more." And he was off again.

Evalynn snickered. "You'd think you'd offered him a free trip to the beach."

I looked at her confused. "Why is he so excited that I like brownies?"

"Because it's something you have in common. He obviously likes you but is trying to find what you like the same."

"Is that important?"

"Sure. You wouldn't ask someone out if you don't have anything in common."

I pondered this. Obviously this was not important at home since Matthew and I had been matched long before our preferences were formed. But here, even food preferences were considered for matching. Austin returned, interrupting my thoughts.

"Let's get back in the water," Austin said after we both had eaten another brownie. I looked at Evalynn and she agreed. The pool was much fuller now so I stayed near the stairs and jumped around a little.

Being in water is tiring. After an hour, I had to get out and had to eat some more. By that time they had hot dogs. Though clearly fake, they were pretty good. Evalynn put all the toppings on it for me to try. That was a little overwhelming. They had chips, baked beans and fruit for the side. I ate it all and finished with another brownie. I decided not to get back in the water. Evalynn wanted to play the game of water volleyball, so I sat on the side and watched. Austin sat in the chair next to me. He talked to me about the game, explaining the rules and scoring system. I listened and asked a couple of questions. It was a little bit exciting, but I did not think this was the way I would want to spend much of my time. Austin was clearly into it and told me about some other sports that sounded about the same.

When the game ended, Evalynn said we needed to go. Austin helped us collect our things and wrapped up two brownies for us.

"See you in the morning, Sarai." He smiled broadly as he handed the food to me.

Once on the road, Evalynn exploded, "Oh my gosh, Sarai. Do you like him or not? I can't read you on this and he is clearly head over heals for you."

"I do like him and I think he could be a good match," I said surprising myself for admitting it out loud.

"So what are you going to do?"

"What do you mean? There is nothing for me to do but wait."

"Clearly you do *not* know how things work out here. If you want to experience dating, tell him you like him. He's probably waiting for you to give him the green light."

I did not understand all of the idioms she used, but I would have to learn them another time. "I am to do what? I do not think that is right. If Austin wants my hand, he needs to ask for it."

"Seriously?" Evalynn looked dumbfounded. "You sound like my dad," she said then laughed. "Of course you sound like him. Anyway, maybe in a perfect world that is how it should work, but this is the real world. Just go for it. Tell him in the morning."

I felt a slight twinge of something that I could not place. I thought momentarily of Matthew, but then reminded myself that he gave me "permission" to experience city life. "I am not sure I could say that to him."

"Then I will. Y'all are so cute together and you said you think you wanna stay here anyway so you don't have to get married. Even if it's just for the summer, at least you'll know."

I felt another twinge but squashed it saying, "I think you may be right. If you would like, you may say something to Austin tomorrow."

Evalynn grinned. "Good!"

*****

As soon as Austin walked in the door at church, Evalynn pounced on him. I stood across the room and watched the interaction with my stomach in knots. I do not even know what I was thinking; my mind simply raced. I saw Austin's eyes get wide and a huge smile spread across his face. Evalynn turned toward me with a shooing motion to him. Austin almost ran to me. He grabbed my hands in his causing my heart to pound.

"Evalynn says that you like me. Is this true?"

He looked deep into my eyes and I looked deeply back. "Yes," was all I could manage. I was so nervous.

"When your brother said you were betrothed I thought you were off limits but you want to be with me? Be my girlfriend?"

"I do not know what that word means, but I do not wish to marry Matthew so I consider myself free to be with you if that is what you desire." I did not know where that sentence came from, but realized I meant it.

"It is!" Austin exclaimed. "So you will go out with me?"

"Of course. Where are we going to go?"

He laughed. "Anywhere. We can decide later." The music began to play and Austin hugged me. It caught me off guard when I wondered why we could not hug and hold hands back home; it was so natural. He took one of my hands and led me to the gathering room. I relaxed a little as it was not as ceremonious as I would have thought. We both grinned from ear to ear and held hands all during the group time.

Now this is love, I thought.

CHAPTER 15

With school being out the teenagers spent a lot of time together so I was able to see Austin almost every day. It was a lot of fun getting to experience new adventures with someone you love.

On Wednesday that first week, I realized I had forgotten to write Matthew when I received a letter from him. I got a small knot in my stomach but commanded it to leave. No matter what he said, I was with Austin.

> My dearest Sarai,
>
> I know you are experiencing a lot in this new culture. Your parents informed me about the situation at church. I feel terrible that Josiah put you in a state of embarrassment, but I know you handled it well. I realize there are other things out there to draw you away. I pray God will guide you and even if it is never, I will wait. You have such a beautiful spirit that I know many will try to win your heart.
>
> Your beloved,
> Matthew

I was unsure what to make of the letter, but I took it as another confirmation that I was free to be with Austin and so I would at the least spend the summer by his side and hoped it would be more than that.

The next week, we went swimming every day. Evalynn insisted that I learn to before we went to camp the next week. By Saturday, I was able to stay up and move in a straight line so she said I would be fine.

Sunday afternoon I packed my small duffel for a week at camp. Needless to say, Evalynn actually chose my clothes, but I put them in the duffle. As I was packing my ink, Evalynn stopped me and handed me a couple of pens and explained them to me. She said I would not want to take an ink well on a trip like this. I took the pens gratefully and was excited at how easy they were to use.

Once packed, I sat to write weekly letters. As I thought about what to write to Joanna, I realized she had not written to me at all. I decided to tell her about swimming, a little of Austin, plans for camp and then asked why she had not written. I told her how much I missed her and that I hoped to hear from her soon.

I debated with myself over what to say to Matthew. I did not know how to respond to what he said so I decided to leave it factual but allowed myself to mention Austin in passing. Maybe I could break it to him over the summer here and there that I had a new betrothed.

I wrote to Mama about camp and how excited I was to learn and spend time with Austin and Evalynn. I told her about learn-ing to swim and hoping to improve over the rest of the summer. I concluded by explaining my feelings over the boys and where I felt like God was leading me here. I asked her to pray for me and that I would be clear in what I heard. A tear ran down my face and onto the paper as I signed it. I touched my hand to my cheek wondering why. I wiped my face. I put my letter in the envelope and prepared it to put in the morning mail.

I heard the dinner call and went quickly upstairs. I pushed the tear out of my mind and enjoyed the rest of my evening.

*****

I awoke at my normal time and the rest of the house stirred not long after. We had to be at the church by 8:00 a.m. to load for the trip to camp. I was told we would leave early to get breakfast out, a tradition for them on trips. I got a chicken biscuit and hash browns and a sweet tea. It was so good I could eat it every day.

We arrived at the church at a quarter 'til eight and some of the leaders were already there packing the luggage of those who had arrived. Evalynn, two of my other cousins and I took our luggage to the trailer and then went to claim our seats on the van. Evalynn and I claimed two rows in our van so Austin and Amberly would have a place to sit when they arrived. I began to get giddy.

Amberly arrived as soon as we emerged from the van. Evalynn grabbed her and put her stuff on the van in her seat. Others came steadily but still no Austin. After twenty minutes, my heart began to pound with worry. Was he not coming? We circled up to pray for the trip, but I could not concentrate on the prayer for wondering. As we closed and said goodbye to the remaining family a car drove into the parking lot. It was he! My heart raced faster and I felt a grin spread on my face. I resisted running to him but waved and showed him which van we would be riding on. I went to make sure there were still two spots. Thankfully no one had moved my things. I sat waiting eagerly for him to come.

And then he was next to me. "Hey, Sarai," Austin said giving me a half hug. "Sorry I'm late."

"I am simply thankful you are here," I said with a smile. "I was really nervous that you would not be coming."

"My brother decided not to pack until this morning making us late." Austin rolled his eyes.

The van started up and the caravan took off down the road. Evalynn and Amberly sat in front of us. Once on the highway, they turned around so we could all talk. They told me about the mountains and the place where we would be staying. They were amazed that I had never been outside of my home until now. They had all been many places. I told them about the traditions of our town and why no one leaves. I explained bethrothal, even though I could not fully explain mine. It was nice to talk about it with people who thought completely differently than my town. I was free to really express myself as well as doubts and frustrations from living in that way. They all listened and sympathized. At some point, Austin reached over and held my hand. His eyes were so kind and his touch so gentle. Thankfully I did not cry.

When I felt I had talked too long, I asked them to talk about something else. They went back to camp and discussed what they planned to do. I expected Austin to release my hand but he did not. I liked the feel of his hand around mine. The longer we sat that way, the more my mind melted away into the thoughts of bliss that would come from a marriage full of love.

Upon arriving at the retreat center, as it was called, we unloaded and went to claim beds. Evalynn and Amberly took a bunk bed and I grabbed a lower bed next to them. The thought of sleeping that high in the air frightened me. We put sheets on our beds and stowed our suitcases underneath.

Once settled, we walked down the path to an old barn that had been fixed into a meeting place. It was odd to see a barn set up like a room, but I liked it. We went to a table where we found out what group we were in for the week and got the schedule. Thankfully Evalynn and I were in the same group, but Amberly had been put in another. They explained to me that they mixed the groups for more variety in each group and to get to know other people not in your grade. I found this strange as, everything at home was done by age.

Others gathered in the barn until Mr. Vaughn called everyone together. He went over the rules and plans, told us the boundaries of the grounds, and gave an overview of what we would be learning. I was excited to be learning more about God for five days and to spend time with Austin. What better combination could there be?

*****

During quiet time Tuesday morning, it dawned on me I had grown lax in reading my Bible daily. It was nice to read quietly while overlooking God's beauty from a porch swing. I also prayed. I prayed God would bring Austin and me closer together that week. I prayed about staying in the city. I prayed for courage to go against my traditional community and do what my heart led me to do. This emboldened me and prepared me, I thought, to learn about God's way for me that week.

We went to breakfast, had a time of worship, and a short message to discuss in our small groups. Though the ages were mixed, we were separated by gender as in Sunday school. I was thankful Mrs. Leland was our group leader. I hoped to talk with her at some point about some of my thoughts and feelings. She led us in a time of discussion and Bible reading, then gave us a couple of questions to think over in some quiet time. I tried but my mind kept going back to Austin and how would life work out for us. Thankfully, I brought my journal so I could write down my thoughts and questions for later.

We had snacks and then went back to large group in the barn. There was another time of worship and a longer word from Pastor Vaughn.

By the time lunch rolled around, I was starving. They switch their meals in the city with lunch being typically lighter than dinner. I looked at my sandwich, bag of chips and glass of soda and knew it would not be enough for an afternoon of play. Evalynn told me to ask for more. I was a bit nervous, but after everyone was served they allowed me to have enough to satisfy my hunger.

After lunch, it was time for the pool. I was excited as I felt like I could actually enjoy playing in the water. Evalynn, Amberly, and I got our suits on and walked to the pool together. Under the hot sun, the water was very refreshing. After getting my whole body wet, I lifted my feet and swam around. I was still a bit awkward at it, but I did not care. There was something freeing about the water and I let myself go in it. I was brought back to reality by someone grabbing my feet. I turned sharply to see Austin grinning at me.

"You're starting to look like a pro," he said.

"I suppose. I still feel clumsy."

"Nah. You look beautiful and graceful." He took my hands and for a moment I thought he would kiss them. Thankfully he did not. "Come on." Austin pulled my hands as he kicked though the water. We swam and splashed, chatted and laughed. It was like we were the only ones there. It was so much fun as we simply enjoyed playing together.

Out of nowhere I thought, *It used to be that way with Matthew.*

The other half of my brain responded, *That was when we were children and we never played like this.*

You did, but only without touching.

That is my point. How can you know someone with whom you cannot fully engage?

And do you know Austin?

"Sarai?" Austin interrupted my inner dialogue. "You okay?"

I did not realize I had stopped swimming and was staring into space. "Yes, I am quite well," I lied. "I was caught in thought about the fun we are having. That is all." I smiled at him. He smiled back and took my hand. We were off again in the water. I suppressed my thoughts on Matthew and intentionally thought about Austin. I would not let Matthew inadvertently wreck my time with Austin or our relationship. He was what I wanted.

*****

The rest of the afternoon and evening were spent with our small group, eating and another time of worship and learning. The next morning had the same schedule. In the afternoon, there was a volleyball tournament between the small groups. There I was given an opportunity to talk with Mrs. Leland.

Sitting next to her on the grass I said, "Mrs. Leland, may I talk to you about something?"

"Sure," she replied with a smile. "What's on your mind?"

I thought for a moment about where to begin. "How did you know you were to marry Mr. Leland?"

"I guess it was common interest and calling," she responded after some thought. "I will say we are not typical. We were both walking closely with the Lord when we met and had little relationship baggage. All of that helped us to see clearly, I believe. The most important thing for us was both of us being called to work with youth."

"Is that important? Where I am from we all do the same thing."

"I think it can be important, but it is not an absolute. For example, you have two people who love the Lord but one is called to teach and the other to office work. Though different they can still work together and so they may be called to lead a class or run a ministry together. But they may not. You have to ask God what He wants you to do. God is the one who created marriage and He is the one who can tell you if you belong together."

I pondered this for a few minutes. Coming from a strictly farming community, I did not really understand this. Mrs. Leland must have seen the confusion on my face, because she then said, "Let me try to simplify what I am saying. For God's plan and purpose will you be better together or apart?"

"That helps, though I do not know if we will be better together or not."

"Who is the 'we'?"

I looked around blushing and whispered, "Austin and me."

"Ah, that's what this is about. I've noticed that y'all are quite close these days."

"Yes, we have become close and I believe that I love him. We have many things in common. He seems to care for me. With him, I finally feel happy." I smiled blushing more.

"Could you explain that?"

"Explain what?"

"Finally feeling happy with him."

"Oh." I hesitated for a moment. How did I explain this? "At home we are betrothed as babies. I am set to marry next May. However, I do not wish to marry my intended. I am not happy at all with the arrangement."

"Why?"

"His family is so strict and traditional. That is not who I am. We have nothing in common except our town. I also desire to truly follow Jesus. Our town is religious, but that is as far as it goes. His family is very religious and does everything 'just so' with tradition as their reasoning."

"What about others in town and your family?"

"My parents believe in a relationship with Jesus and teach us such at home. We do follow traditions, but they seek God first, or strive to do so. No one else does that as far as I know. We are different."

"So you wouldn't be happy with anyone there is what you're saying?"

"I do not believe I would be."

"What do you think the purpose of marriage is?"

"I am still unsure. Where I come from, it is to keep home and have children."

"I will help you through this one, but I want to show you Scripture and I did not bring my Bible down here. So let me ask you another question. Do you really know what your betrothed believes or do you make assumptions based on his family?"

"A woman would never question a man's faith." My answer surprised me a little, but I realized it was the thought of my culture. "That is what our town teaches."

"Well, if he is to be your husband, you should be able to ask him. Pray about it and if God leads, ask your betrothed what he believes. At least then you will be sure."

I thought about this. I wasn't sure I liked the idea. Did I want to be sure about Matthew? I wanted to stay in the city where adults can have fun and I can make decisions and possibly learn more and do more. And I wanted to be with Austin who clearly wanted me. I finally looked at Mrs. Leland in the eyes, "I will consider this."

She looked me in the eyes very seriously and said, "I also want you to consider this, happiness is not the most important thing."

CHAPTER 16

The conversation with Mrs. Leland weighed on me the rest of the day and into the next. I prayed here and there, but not seriously. I just wanted to stay in the city with Austin and do what I wanted to do. That was all. The battle inside me was intense; swords clashing as I went back and forth between staying where I felt safe and wanting to risk tradition but finding out there was still something for me at home.

Thursday afternoon we had some free time when Austin and I decided to hang out alone. Since this idea of asking about beliefs was on my mind, I decided to try it on Austin before deciding if I would dare to ask Matthew about his.

There was a creek in the woods by the camp. Hand in hand, we walked to a nearby part and found a grassy spot on which to sit. Face-to-face, he took my hands again as we talked lightly for a while. A lull came in the conversation so I mustered my strength and asked, "Austin, what do you believe?"

Austin looked me in the eyes with some confusion. "What do I believe about what?"

I thought the question was obvious so I said, "Your beliefs."

"You mean about God?" he asked.

"Yes!" I almost shouted. I had expected this to be easier.

I guess he thought the answer was obvious because Austin simply responded, "Well, I believe in God."

This conversation seemed to already be going in a circle. How would I do this in a letter? "And?"

"And what?" Austin responded almost perturbed.

This, in turn, frustrated me. "What do you believe about God?" I almost yelled.

He dropped my hands unexpectedly and crossed his arms. He looked at me suspiciously, as if I was trying to trick him. This was making me nervous as I did not want to anger him, but it also made me seriously question how Matthew would respond. "I don't know what you are getting at, Sarai. I believe in God. I am a Christian. What else do you think there is? Isn't that what you believe?"

I had not expected that to be his response. That is essentially how I expected Matthew to respond, only with authority and no question to me. I also realized I had not shared my faith with him assuming he believed as my cousins and I did. I took a moment to think before looking at Austin in the eyes and saying, "I believe Jesus is the Son of God and that He died for me."

Austin relaxed a little at that statement and said, "Oh that. Yeah, I believe that."

"Then why did you not say so?"

"Because most people are just trying to figure out your religion when they ask those kinds of questions."

"I do not understand. Either you are a Christian or not."

"No, it's not that simple. There are many other religions."

"I did not know this." I found myself intrigued. I had never heard this even in history studies, though I am not surprised those in our town would try to hide it if they knew it to be true. After a moment, I tucked this thought away and went back to the question at hand. "I want to be sure I understand you, do you believe in Jesus?"

Austin smiled and replied, "Yes," taking my hands again. "Now let's talk about something else." He went on to talk about sports or something. I do not really remember now. I was too busy thinking with only half my mind there.

At dinner time we returned to camp hand in hand. I saw Evalynn and Amberly watching us closely as we returned. They stood behind us in the dinner line and made small talk with us. I could see they wanted to know what had happened but dared not to ask in front of Austin. I knew I would get pounced on later.

*****

And it came as we were getting ready for bed.

"What happened this afternoon?" Evalynn said jumping next to me on my bed.

"Yeah, tell us all the details," Amberly said jumping on my other side.

I looked back and forth at them for a minute not knowing what to say. Their big eyes and wide grins said they thought we had done something we ought not, so I simply said, "We walked down to the creek and talked."

Their faces fell. "That's all?" Amberly said. "I thought he'd have tried to make a move by now."

"Make a move?" I questioned.

"Yeah, like kiss you. I know he wants to." Amberly grinned again and raised her eyebrows.

"That is allowed?"

"Why not? It's part of the dating process. How else will you know if your feelings are real?"

This was almost too much for me. I understood holding hands and hugging, but not anything else. I saw that as for marriage. "I would not let him. That should be for your wedding day. Do you not think so?"

Amberly looked around before answering softly, "Sex is for your wedding day, but everything else is up for grabs, er, you can do."

I looked at Evalynn with a plea for help. She smiled and shook her head. "I wouldn't go that far, Amberly, but there's nothing wrong with kissing. The Bible says to greet each other with a kiss and we are family. Makes sense to me."

My head was swimming and I had no time to sort it out as we would be returning "home" the next day. They asked me about our conversation, and Amberly thought I was nuts for caring so much about the specifics of his beliefs.

"We're all Christian," she threw out there.

I was done. I told them I wanted to go to sleep. I could not handle anymore. Lying down on my pillow, I prayed in my head, "Lord, who is right? The ideas seem so extreme, but that would be true freedom and you have set us free." I then admitted to myself that I did desire to kiss Austin but had denied it, thinking it was sin. And to add to my confusion, the idea of other religions blew me away. I found it hard to sleep as my mind raced, but eventually the racing led to a much needed crash.

*****

I awoke just as the sun began to peek in the window. Everyone else was snoring so I took my journal out on the porch for a few minutes of writing reflection before the rest of the world awoke. Sitting on a rocking chair, a light breeze blew into my face as I thought about the previous day. Silently I prayed for wisdom and wrote:

> *What does all this mean? I love a Christian man who does not openly speak what he believes without prompting. I am engaged to a "Christian" man who does not share what he believes. Both are silent in different ways. I guess I must ask Matthew to know for sure what he believes. If he is not a believer I cannot marry him. It would be unwise. However even after asking I am uncertain as to what Austin fully believes. Is that any better? Oh Lord, why am I so tormented with questions now? I was certain of Austin and now he may be as Matthew is to me spiritually. But Austin does adore me and makes me happy. Mrs. Leland says happiness is not the most important thing but surely You want Your people to be happy. I am beyond confused.*

My eyes closed as tears welled behind my lids. The city was supposed to be the answer, not more questions. Austin was supposed to be the true love, not an option. At that point, I felt not only torn between two worlds but torn between these two boys, like my heart and soul were dividing. Maybe I should have never left. A hand on my shoulder startled me.

"I'm sorry, Sarai. Didn't mean to scare you." Mrs. Leland smiled at me. "Are you okay?" Her voice was so kind and gentle, like Mama's. Oh, how I wanted Mama.

I tried to smile and fake a yes, but she already saw the tears. I shook my head as I looked down. Mrs. Leland took my hands and began to pray quietly for my comfort and peace. When she finished, I smiled and hugged her. "That is what Mama would have done," Mrs. Leland said nothing but held me as I cried lightly. I began to hear movement in the cabin and sat up. "Thank you."

Mrs. Leland smiled. "Call me when you're ready to talk more at home. I'll take you for lunch one day." I nodded with a forced smile. "Let's go get breakfast."

*****

I did my best to pretend I was fine during the drive. I smiled and let Austin hold my hand. Joining the conversation was still a challenge since they talked about things I was not familiar with. But I listened and my mind turned.

This week had shown me how different I was, at least where I came from. I was homesick. I had not believed it would happen, but all I wanted in that moment was my house, my bed and the simplicity of not knowing that things could be different.

CHAPTER 17

As soon as we got back to the house, Aunt Dianne grabbed our suitcases and began washing clothes. I had forgotten that the next week
Samuel had a break from classes and we would all be going to the
beach. I helped sort the clothes and start a first load before slipping
down to my room to write Mama. I debated about what to write and
how much to say, but as I put my quill to my parchment, which I had
also missed, the words flowed:

> Oh, Mama,
>
> My heart is confused and torn. I am
> so thankful for the opportunity Papa and
> you have given me, but at this moment, I
> want to take it back. In some ways, I love
> it here, but in many I am realizing I do not
> believe this is who I am. But I am not sure
> home is who I am either. Who am I, Mama?
> I am being torn in two. Two worlds. Two
> people. And none of it is what I thought. I
> feel so lost. I know I should not come home
> yet, but today I desire it, if nothing else to
> have you hold me and tell me all will be
> right. I am grateful for Mrs. Leland. She is
> much like you and has been a great com-
> fort to me this week past. I do not wish to
> burden you, Mama, but my heart is crying

out and I know you will understand and
know best how to pray. I miss you, Mama.
Kiss all the children for me.

Much Love,
Sarai

I moved my head to late and a tear caught my name. I patted it dry, but the evidence was still there. I worried that it would burden Mama more but left it instead of rewriting.

I got up to go outside when Evalynn stopped me. "What's going on with you?"

Turning slowly, I looked at her and said, "I am not sure I know."

"Why are you crying? You've been all but crying all day."

"Because my heart is split and I do not know that it can be repaired."

Evalynn looked at me funny but said nothing else. I turned to go outside.

*****

The summer sun blazed down on my back as I walked down the street, my mind racing with thoughts that came from all directions. Tears burned my eyes and ran down my face, but I could not pin point why. I wanted to scream. I wanted to run. Without thinking my feet sped up, faster and faster. I didn't know where I was going I just wanted to out run my thoughts. I couldn't tell you how much time passed or how far I went but my body finally gave out. A scream escaped my lips as I collapsed on some grass and sobbed. Had I known this was where this adventure would take me I would have stayed home and simply lived a wondering life. This was far too painful.

I heard a car drive up next to me. The car door opened and closed and arms embraced me. It was Amelia. She said nothing but helped me to my unstable feet and put me in the car. My body shook the whole way home. Amelia held me as Samuel drove. She stroked my hair. I tried to relax, but it didn't work. I felt the car stop. Silence abounded with unspoken words between Samuel and Amelia before Samuel got out of the car. My body was still shaking though starting to lessen. Amelia continued to stroke my head as I willed my body to stop shaking.

When only my hands trembled, Amelia finally spoke, "What is the matter, Sarai? Why are you so troubled?"

"I am not sure, Amelia," I answered. "My mind is my enemy right now."

"How do you mean?" Her voice was tender.

I did not think there was any way she would understand, but I decided to try and explain. "I so desired to come here, to the city. I still believe it is the answer to my problem, but I am so confused. Right now I wish I had stayed at home, remaining ignorant of another way of life. Now I feel divided. There are things I love about home, but I love things here as well. Who am I now? Where do I belong?" I looked down at my hands. My words were going in circles and I didn't feel like saying anymore.

Amelia sat quietly like she was thinking. She said, "You are who God made you, like you have always been. That has not changed. Who that is, specifically, God and you will work it out together. But you must let Him guide you. As to where you belong I cannot say. What problem do you believe is being answered here?"

My heart began to race, my hands became clammy, and a lump formed in my throat. I had said more than I intended. I forgot that Amelia did not know my doubts as Samuel and Matthew were close friends. "Oh, it is nothing." I tried to stay calm and hold my voice steady.

I waited for her to press in on me, but she simply said, "All right. If you need to talk, let me know."

I tried to look Amelia in the eyes, but I could not. I didn't know why I felt ashamed or why I could not admit my feelings to her, but I stayed silent and nodded. We sat a few more moments before Amelia opened the door and helped me out.

*****

Showers are great. Hot showers come straight from heaven. I was so thankful for a hot shower that day. I sat in the shower, the water beating on my back as I hugged my knees. I was out of tears but I still cried. I did not know what I was feeling or why I was crying still. I just wanted it to stop.

When the shower started to run cold, I got out. Time had escaped me and I realized the sun was beginning to set. I had meant to help with dinner and laundry. No one had come to get me. They must have realized I needed to be alone. I wasn't even hungry. Some of my clothes were folded on the bed. Without looking at them, I put them back in my suitcase and curled up in bed. I thought about writing Matthew. It terrified me, but I decided that if I was going to get any answers to my confused questions I had to ask him his beliefs. I realized I was basing everything on assumption. At least if I had the facts I would know exactly what my options were.

*****

In the morning, my brain continued where it left off when I went to sleep. I was trying to decide how to word my letter to Matthew. Before getting my parchment and quill, I prayed silently and asked God to give me the words. Sitting at the desk my hand wrote,

> Dear Matthew,
> I realize what I am about to write is quite unconventional, but I have some questions that I need answered. I do not desire to disrespect you. Therefore I ask you not to take it as such. Matthew, I need to know what you believe in your heart of hearts. Please tell me all you believe for I want to know all. Thank you for your patience and understanding.
>
> Love,
> Sarai

I stared at the letter as it dried and read it over in my mind. My hands worked to fold the letter, put it in an envelope, and address it as my eyes continued to stare. Still in a daze, I walked to get a stamp and take the letter to the mailbox. I heard noises around me, but it was not until I returned to the house that my brain responded to the stimuli. Thankfully no one addressed my mood. I ate breakfast and willed myself out of my pensive state, determined to reserve my thoughts until I was alone again.

Forcing a smile, I talked with the family as we ate. After breakfast I helped with the dishes and helped around the house to prepare to leave the next day. Honestly, doing work helped me to feel better. I did not realize how much I missed doing stuff in the house. It gave me purpose and something else to think about.

After dinner, I packed my bag for the beach and took my bag to Uncle Mark to put in the car. The day had made me more excited about the vacation and rejuvenated my spirit.

CHAPTER 18

Seeing Austin at church the next morning brought distraction. Throughout Sunday school and church, I had to fight to focus. It felt like it would not end. As soon as the service let out, we piled in the cars and headed out of town.

The girls rode in the van. I stared out of the window and listened to the chatter as the scenes whirled by. After lunch, I loosened up a bit and began to add the occasional comment. When Aunt Dianna started a sing along, I could not help but laugh. She sang everything from kids' songs to '80s rock. I knew none of them except the two hymns she sang for my benefit. The more she sang, the more I laughed. Who knew there were so many silly songs out there? We sing only to worship. Frivolous songs would be seen as a waste of time and dishonoring to God. I loved it. I wanted to learn them all. Evalynn said she would teach me. I love to sing, especially praise songs, but learning that you could sing about anything increased the passion for it.

We arrived at the beach as the sun set. It seemed beautiful but it was almost dark. I would have to wait a day to experience the full beauty of the beach. I was tired anyway.

Uncle Mark had rented a large beach house for us to stay in. It was not quite as big as his home, but there was still plenty of space. Evalynn, Denise, and I took one room. I was so thankful Jonathan volunteered to sleep on the sofa so all five of the girls would not have to share a room. They let me have a double bed to myself and shared the other. Who needed that much space to sleep? We settled in our beds and attempted to get to sleep early. This was in vain, for every time there was silence someone would start to sing followed by laughter. This went well into the night until we finally drifted off to sleep.

*****

I was so thankful that even with a late night I awoke before the sun. Evalynn told me the sunrise over the ocean was beautiful. I thought about waking her but decided she could see it another morning. I slipped on my shoes and headed downstairs. The light was just beginning to peak through the windows. I went to the kitchen to grab some juice and realized the ocean was literally in the backyard. I stood staring in awe. There was nothing close to this at home. We had a lake and a few small ponds here and there, but to look and see nothing but black water was breathtaking.

Forgetting my juice, I walked out of the back door, down the stairs and directly into the sand. I removed my shoes shoving my toes into the sand. It was so gritty, but somehow enjoyable. Walking slowly toward the water my mind did not even try to race. I felt at peace and I wanted to stay here. Could this kind of peace and tranquility remain forever?

The sun continued to creep up over the water, shimmering across the waves. The waves. It took me awhile to notice them. The sound was so soothing. Eventually my feet reached the water and the lapping hit my ankles. It was cold and refreshing. Time really stood still as I took in all of the new sensations. There came a light breeze. I shut my eyes as it blew across my face. I pulled my hair down and held my arms out. My hair and clothes rustled. I felt as if I would fly away. There was something special about this place. That's when I heard the still, small voice, "Trust Me. Stop thinking so much about what ifs and pay attention. I will make your steps clear."

I thought of Mama's Christmas present lying on the bed upstairs. "Trust in God" is what I slept on every night and I still was struggling to really trust Him. But what was I supposed to pay attention to? How I wished God would just appear in front of me and clearly say what I was to do. The voice said again, "Stop," so gently that my mind did and simply took in the breeze and the moment of quiet beauty.

"Breathtaking, is it not?" Samuel said quietly.

"Yes, it is very beautiful," I said without starting.

"I came here at Thanksgiving with our relatives. It was not as enjoyable then." Samuel paused looking calmly over the ocean. I could tell something was on his mind but waited patiently. After several moments of watching the sun together, he turned to me and said, "I have been wanting to talk with you, Sarai, but until now the timing has been poor."

I nodded seriously and said, "I am listening."

Samuel tensed a little and looked back out at the ocean before saying, "I know you have been struggling, Sarai. You are clearly in turmoil. Why have you not come to me?" He looked at me with sad eyes. I had no idea I had hurt him.

A lump formed in my throat as I realized this and decided how honest I should be with him. Since he was already hurting I decided it would be better to be completely honest and get all of the damage out of the way. I looked down at my wringing hands and said, "I did not come to you because Matthew is your best friend. I did not think you would understand, and that you would tell me all the reasons why I should marry Matthew and that I am foolish for my feelings."

Lifting my chin, he said, "I could tell you all the reasons why you should marry Matthew and that you are foolish for your feelings but I will not. There have been many times recently that I have wanted to send you home and command you to marry Matthew, but I am learning that is not the way of love. Love allows room for mistakes and growth. It does not demand an action right away. Love is patient and kind. Most of all it is an act of the will. It is not a feeling. You are my sister, Sarai, and I care for you deeply. I want God's best for you."

Tears rolled down my face as my brother spoke. His words were so beautiful and deep down I knew them to be true. But my feelings still raged inside of me. A part of me wanted to bear all to Samuel, the other part was still afraid. I knew he could sense it.

"Sarai, please tell me what is going on in your heart," Samuel said. "I want to help you." He relaxed a little and a small smile appeared on his face.

I wiped my eyes and looked back at Samuel. "I am still struggling to put all of the words to it, but it is primarily a battle of worlds. I miss home and I like it here. My heart is torn. I am sad to think if I choose home, I cannot come back and if I choose here, I cannot go home." I stopped there.

"And what of the boy?" Samuel was direct.

The lump in my throat grew. Tears formed again. Could I admit to Samuel my feelings. "I…" the words caught in my throat. I looked down again. "I believe I love Austin. I want to marry him."

I waited for a reaction, but it did not come. When I looked back at Samuel, his eyes were downcast and looking out at the waves.

"Samuel, please do not be angry with me. This is why I did not wish to tell you."

Now it was my brother who had tears. I was surprised to see them and my heart broke. I touched his arm and he looked back at me.

Samuel let out a deep sigh. "I am not angry with you, Sarai. I am sad that you feel that way. Just as Joanna and you have been waiting to be sisters, so Matthew and I have waited to be brothers. Thinking that that may never happen causes me great sadness." He paused and looked back at the ocean again. He was clearly wrestling with what to say next. Letting out another sigh, he turned to me and said, "Do you know if Austin feels the same?"

I did not quite understand the question. "Why would he not? He has been pursuing me since I arrived. What else would it mean?"

"I am not saying this to cause you to change your mind but simply to help you understand how things are here." Another deep sigh. "People here do not view relationships as we do. If they are attracted to someone, they start the relationship, and if it fails, they end it. There is no guarantee of marriage."

I was surprised to hear that. The idea was foreign. "How do they decide to marry?"

"The boy and girl decide. Sometimes the parents are involved, but in general it is decided between the two who will marry."

"How do I find out what Austin expects?"

"You must ask him?"

There I was again in another situation where I must ask a male about something. It was so odd. "How do I ask him? I know nothing of asking men questions, Samuel. You know this."

"Simply ask him if he intends to marry you."

We heard Amelia call from the house, "Samuel, Sarai, breakfast is ready."

"We will be there in a moment," Samuel called back. To me, he said, "It is all right to ask questions when you need to know something. I would plan the timing well and be careful of tone, but ask. You need to know. If necessary, tell him I am forcing you to ask."

I smiled at that though my heart raced. Samuel motioned toward the house. We turned and walked together. It then occurred to me to ask him, "Has Amelia heard from Joanna?"

I saw Samuel twinge, "Yes. She is well."

"Why do you look as if something is wrong?"

He forced a smile. "She is well. You should ask Amelia if you would like to know more."

My heart raced faster, thinking something may be wrong with my friend but I said no more. We washed our feet on the porch and went in for breakfast.

*****

Amelia made a hearty breakfast all on her own. I scolded her again for not getting me to help her but she insisted it was fine and said I could make breakfast tomorrow.

Evalynn commanded me to hurry with my bathing suit. She did not want to miss a minute of the sand and sun. I dressed as quickly as possible and grabbed my towel and we ran as fast as we could outside. The rest of the family was not far behind.

We laid out towels, then ran to the water. Evalynn bade me to swim in the ocean as she came up for air, but the thought of drowning made me stay in waist deep water with my feet firmly planted. I splashed and walked around for a while, but soon I was bored and headed back to the towels only half wet.

"Don't wanna swim?" Aunt Dianne asked.

I shook my head. "I am not very confident in the water. I am afraid I would get too far and drown."

Aunt Dianna smiled sweetly. "I understand. I learned to swim as an adult and the ocean makes me nervous too."

"Water is for bathing," Amelia chimed in. "I think the ocean is beautiful, but I want my feet on dry ground."

We all laughed. The guys had teamed up with some others and were playing volleyball nearby. I wanted to try but decided to ask later when the females could play. Instead I talked with Aunt Dianna and Amelia. I also played with the sand letting it run through my fingers. It was fascinating but I could not figure out why.

Aunt Dianna excused herself and I realized my opportunity to talk to Amelia. "Amelia, I have been meaning to ask you, have you heard from Joanna?"

Amelia made a face almost identical to Samuel's expression earlier. "I have and she is well."

"But something is wrong, I can see it in your eyes. Please tell me what is wrong."

"It is time to go to lunch. Aunt Dianna said we need to leave at eleven," Amelia said.

"I do not need to eat. I need to know about my friend."

"I understand, but we do not have time currently. Please, let us talk later."

"Amelia, you have me quite worried. Please, tell me now."

Amelia in her calm manner said, "I want to talk later. After dinner, we will come watch the sunset and talk. Do not be afraid. I promise she is well."

I tried to breathe deeply to slow my heart. I was so anxious. My mind raced. "Why are they saying she is well yet look as if she is ill? What is wrong with my dearest friend?"

Aunt Dianna called us all to get ready for lunch. They gave me a dress to put over my bathing suit. I was thankful it was long. I put on flip flops which felt odd. Apparently we were walking down the beach to a beach side restaurant.

At eleven on the dot, we left from our back steps. Evalynn, Amelia, and I talked about the beauty of the beach while Amelia and I learned the names of things we had never seen before. It was fascinating. Evalynn suggested we take pictures so we could remember. It sounded like fun, but we were being rushed along by the hungry men. We decided to take some on the way back.

The restaurant was quite literally on the beach. There was a small building that I assumed was the kitchen surrounded by a concrete slab on all sides with tables and chairs. We walked up and the host told us to move the tables however we needed. As we settled, he brought menus. It might as well have been another language. The only things I recognized were fish and fries. Evalynn told me what she liked and we each ordered a dish to share.

The seafood was quite different from the game I was use to and even from the food I had been introduced to in the city, but it wasn't bad. I particularly enjoyed the jumbo shrimp and crab cakes.

Walking home, Evalynn taught Amelia and me how to capture what we were seeing in photographs. She told us we could take as many as we wanted and so we did. They were not great but we had fun. It helped to keep my mind from exploding with questions.

When we arrived at the house, we took some pictures of us. Uncle Mark took a cousins picture and Samuel took one of Uncle Mark's family. We took silly shots and serious ones. It was so much fun.

During the heat of the day, we went inside to watch a movie and look at the pictures we had taken. I ended up falling asleep on the sofa and had a nice hour-long nap.

I awoke just as Amelia was beginning dinner so I ran to the kitchen to help. She told me what we were making and I began my portion. It was then my mind began to run again. I wanted to ask Amelia what was going on with Joanna but I refrained. My mind spun with possibilities and as my mind spun the more distracted I became. Before I knew what was happening, my hand was on fire from water boiling over. I screamed and Amelia turned on the faucet to run lukewarm water on my hand. The burning relinquished for a minute and then changed to a rushing burn as my blood rushed to the effected skin. It was red but only minor. Samuel went to the store to get ointment, gauze, and tape. Amelia excused me from the kitchen and Aunt Dianna went to help.

"Are you okay?" Evalynn asked while I held my hand.

I forced a smile. "It is not the first time. It is only a little sore. I will be all right once Samuel gets it bandaged."

"You are brave." Evalynn shook her head. "I would be freaking out right now."

"To overreact would make it worse. I need to relax and hold my hand."

Evalynn nodded and offered to replay the movie for me to help me relax. I told her it was fine to play it though I did not understand how it would help me relax.

The rest of the evening crawled by. Finally around eight, Amelia motioned for me to join her outside. There were two chairs perfectly aligned to watch the setting sun. Though beautiful and picturesque, I was much too concerned about Joanna to thoroughly enjoy it as I ought.

Amelia and I sat in silence for a moment. I could not tell if she was waiting on herself or me. As I breathed in to ask about Joanna, Amelia took my unburned hand and looked at me. Her eyes had a hint of tears. "I was hoping to wait until after vacation to tell you about this, but since you have asked, Samuel and I decided it would be best to tell you now." My heart was racing. "Just before you left for camp, I received a letter from Joanna. She is so upset. Josiah went home and told her his version of what happened between Austin and you and told her not to write to you."

All of my blood left my hand and rushed to my face. Tears welled like they never had before. My heart almost ripped in two. How could he do that to me? I had lost my closest brother and now my best friend. Why had I come here?

"There is more," Amelia interrupted my thoughts. My heart ached. "Josiah has asked her to give the letters you send Joanna to him to read." My heart stopped. "She has agreed."

"Why would she do that?" I blurted out without thought. "She is my best friend. I thought I could trust her!" The tears poured. I tried to remember what I had written. A lump grew in my throat as I thought about what I had said concerning Austin. What would Josiah do with the letters? What was happening to my family? What was happening to me?

Amelia put her arm around me and drew me close. I cried hard and waited for her to say something but she didn't. I wanted her to answer my questions but she didn't. I composed myself and looked into Amelia's eyes. "Why is Joanna doing this?"

"Joanna seems to be afraid. She is as confused as you are. She, too, is trying to understand what is happening to her best friend, and the only person she believes she can trust is Josiah. Her betrothed is who has come home. She wonders if you will come home."

"I will be home in a month."

"Yes, but for how long?"

I thought about this. How long would I be home? My only options were a year or forever. Why did I have to make a lifelong decision now?

"Must I decide that now? How do I decide?"

"No, you have time to decide. I cannot tell you how either. I am here because of my husband. If you would like, I can give you my opinion, but really it needs to be what you believe is best."

"How do I know what is best?"

"Pray without ceasing."

I leaned onto Amelia's shoulder and stared at the ocean. What was I going to do? How was I going to decide? I thought about my conversation with Samuel at sunrise and realized that asking Austin about his intentions was the only logical next step. I wanted to call him so I would know right away, but I knew I needed to see his face. I prayed for my mind to calm and focused on the setting sun. I marveled at the beauty in front of me until I started to doze. It was time for bed.

CHAPTER 19

I was thankful to get all of my serious conversations completed the first day of vacation. My mind would wander and I wrote about the conversations and my wandering thoughts in my journal throughout the week. I did my best to limit the time I did this so I could enjoy being with the family during our activities.

Overall, I was able to enjoy the week. We went to a nearby pool a couple of times so everyone could swim. I tried many types of seafood. One day we went to an amusement park and I went on many of the rides. Evalynn tried to get me to ride the roller coasters that went upside down, but the ones that didn't messed with my stomach, so I passed. Mostly I enjoyed the sun and being outside.

*****

During the trip home, we had another sing along. We talked a little about the differences between the city and our town. I began to wonder if I should ask Uncle Mark's opinion about my potential quick decision. A year is quick, right? I reminded myself I should still talk to Austin first and go from there. The biggest question was did I warn him of the need to have a deep discussion. Second was where to talk. Everything we had done was in a group setting. I was not sure about going somewhere alone, but I did not want to talk at church or around a bunch of nosey people. I prayed for it to be clear and for the time to be soon.

*****

We arrived at the house around dinner time. Aunt Dianna ordered pizza while the men unloaded the car. We had a week and a half before the mission trip with the church youth group so we did not need to start laundry right away. Instead, we watched a movie and ate pizza. I opted for bed as soon as the movie ended.

*****

I did my best to act normally when I saw Austin on Sunday morning. We hugged. He asked about vacation and I shared my experiences. He wanted to take me back to an amusement park and take me on an upside down roller coaster. I smiled at the thought of us holding hands while the sky raced under our feet. And that was when he said, "My family is going on Thursday. I bet my parents would let you come with us."

"I will ask Samuel if I can come with you."

"Great. How 'bout after church."

I nodded as the music began and we went to our seats.

*****

After church, Austin made sure it was all right with his parents for me to join them on Thursday. I was surprised when Samuel said I could go. After our conversation, I thought he would say no way, but he gave his blessing since it was a family event and not the two of us alone.

Evalynn was so excited that I was going on a date with Austin. At home she told me I would have to have the perfect outfit and went through all our clothes. She suggested I wear my bathing suit under my clothes for the water rides. She tried to talk me into wearing pants, but I still did not find them comfortable. I had a mid-calf looser skirt that I thought would be best and she lent me a T-shirt that she said was cute and better for a day outside. Evalynn then played with my hair to find a good hairstyle. I did not understand all the fuss, but it was nice having my hair brushed, so I just let her.

"Are you excited for Thursday?" Evalynn asked as she braided.

"I have a funny feeling in my stomach when I think about it. I think that means I am." I smiled to myself.

"Sounds like it to me. There are great rides and lots of time to hold hands. Maybe he'll kiss you."

This startled me. "He would kiss me in front of his parents?"

Evalynn laughed. "No, you probably will not spend half the time with his parents. They'll let you do whatever."

I didn't know what to do with that information. Should I be excited or concerned? There would be lots of people around so we wouldn't ever be completely alone. Maybe we would be able to talk. The nerves hit. What am I going to say? How did I ask him about his intentions? Should I get Evalynn's advice? No, she would ask why it mattered. I was thankful I had four days to figure it out.

Evalynn said she figured out how to do my hair just as Aunt Dianna called us to eat. We ran upstairs and joined the family at the table.

*****

When you are waiting for something, time seems to crawl. That week I wished I had the ability to sleep until noon so the days would go by quicker. But alas, I woke with the sun.

Wednesday afternoon, I received a letter from Matthew. My heart raced as I thought about the letter I sent. I went to my desk and closed the door. My hands shook as I opened the envelope. There was a lot of parchment to read.

> My dearest Sarai,
>
> Thank you for your last letter. I am grateful that even though it is unconventional, you are brave enough to ask tough

questions. I am not completely sure what all you desire to know so I will address everything that I can think to write about my beliefs.

I will not record everything he said, but he went through the Bible and explained what he believed with Scripture references. My eyes watered as I read and saw he believed what I did. Why had he never told me this before? After the long list, he wrote,

I so do appreciate the opportunity to share my heart with you. Please forgive me for not expressing this well before, nor asking you about your heart. I still have much to learn about caring for another's soul. I await your next letter, and if you feel as if you are able to share, I would like to know what you believe in your heart of hearts.

Your beloved,
Matthew

The tears were flowing. What was I to do with this? His response was supposed to make my decision easier, not harder. "God, why does he have to believe the same things? Why is he not like everyone else in his heart? How do I choose in this? What is the right thing to do?"

I read the letter again and then again. I knew I had no choice but to ask Austin his intentions as soon as possible. It was the last piece of information I needed to know what was truly best.

*****

I was wide awake at dawn. Amelia was right behind me in the kitchen and helped me start breakfast. Even with the conveniences, we mostly cooked from scratch.

"Are you ready for today?" Amelia asked with a smile.

"I believe that I am. I really cannot say." My voice caught a little.

"Is everything all right?"

"I will hopefully find out today."

"What do you mean?"

"If we have some time to talk in a mostly private place, I will ask Austin about his intentions. I am nervous about doing this since it is unthinkable for us."

Amelia stopped and hugged me. She prayed a short prayer for strength and wisdom over me.

"Thank you, Amelia." I considered telling her what Matthew revealed in his letter, but I decided to wait until I talked to Austin. We finished breakfast in a long silence.

I was ready at 8:30 a.m. on the dot. Evalynn woke up early to make sure my hair was done perfectly. As Samuel left for class, he said, "Have a good day, Sarai. Be wise. I am praying for you."

Austin's family pulled in the driveway a little before nine. It took a minute before he got out and came to the door. He told me I looked great, and we walked to the car together.

The amusement park was far bigger than the one at the beach and was a lot fuller. We waited in line half an hour to get tickets and go in. Austin's brothers had also brought friends, so, as Evalynn predicted, we were free to go and do what we wanted. Each pair was given food money, and we were released until 8:00 p.m.!

Austin told me he had the day mapped out. He took my hand and walked to the back of the park. We talked about the different rides and what they were like. His plan was to ride them all.

Austin was kind enough to plan some of the easier rides first before taking me on a normal roller coaster. With all the walking and standing in line, it did not take me long to get hungry. He wanted to wait a little longer for lunch, so we got a jumbo soft pretzel. It was pretty good, but very salty.

After a couple more rides, he told me it was time to try going upside down. He bribed me with lunch right after. My stomach churned as we waited in line. I felt like I might be sick as we got in our seats. The worker checked to make sure we were in securely. Austin held my hand and said, "Don't be scared. It's fun." A minute later, we were out of the station and climbing the first hill. I squeezed Austin's hand hard as we flew down the track. It was terrifying and yet somehow exhilarating. My stomach was still stirring as the car pulled into the house, but for some reason, I wanted to do it again. Austin was thrilled to hear that, but I reminded him I needed to eat lunch.

I thought that it would have been a good time to talk, but the lunch places were packed so we ate and talked about other things. We went on more rides for three hours before getting another snack. We got some really yummy ice cream. We sat down in the ice cream parlor and saw only a couple other people. I decided with the day coming to an end it was now or never.

I took a deep breath and said, "Austin, I must ask you something."

"Okay." He only looked slightly concerned.

I breathed deeply again. "What are your intentions with our relationship?"

He had a weird look on his face. "My intentions? What do you mean?"

I didn't expect him not to understand. "Your intentions. I do not know another word. It is what I know."

"Can you give me a definition?"

I thought for a minute before saying, "What is your purpose in pursuing me?"

"My purpose?" Austin looked even more perplexed. "I don't know. I guess to get to know you better. That's the purpose of dating anyway."

"And after you get to know me better, what is next?"

His confusion grew. "I really don't understand. Is there supposed to be something next?"

It would have felt better if he had stabbed me in the heart. Austin had had no thought of marriage at all. Did I dare ask him? I really had no choice at that point.

"Well, my assumption would be marriage." The words crawled out of my mouth.

Austin's eyes grew to the size of saucers. "Marriage?" He choked on the word. "I am nowhere near thinking about that. I have to graduate from high school, go to college, get a job. I mean, I've got at least five years before I could get married, realistically."

He said I. Another knife in the heart. He said five years. Could I actually wait that long? I knew I could not express my own desires and feelings at that point, so I asked, "If you cannot be married for at least five years, then why pursue me?"

It was clear he had not really thought about this. He stammered, "I don't know. I guess because you are beautiful and seemed interesting. When you said you were free, I figured I'd go for it to see what you were like. Why did you want to be with me?"

This was easier for me. "You have shown a genuine interest in me and pursued me in affection. You are fun and willing to talk to someone who is different from you and showed some respect for my culture. Mostly, with your persistence in getting to know me, I thought you desired to be married." I looked down as I finished my statement and blushed.

Austin took my hands in his and waited for me to look at him. Once we made eye contact, he said, "Sarai, you're so nice and really beautiful. You're different from girls here which adds to the attraction. I'm not saying I wouldn't want to marry you in the future, but I can't make a decision like that now. I mean, I'm seventeen."

I began to tear up but forced them back so I could speak. "I do not have the option of waiting five years. When I finish school in May, I must marry Matthew or leave for good."

"Then just come back here." Austin made it sound so easy. "Like I said, I'm not saying no. I'm saying I don't know right now. A lot can happen in five years."

I nodded at him. "I understand," I said, though I really didn't.

"Let's not think about it right now. We have more rides to go on and just a couple hours left."

Not think about it? How did he not see the seriousness of the situation? We finished our ice cream and I tried not to think about our conversation. Austin brought up other things and tried to share some more interests. I faked a smile and let him hold my hand as we walked around the rest of the park. I enjoyed a couple of the rides we had left but mostly faked my enjoyment as well.

At eight, we met the rest of his family at the exit gate. I was exhausted in every way possible and was ready to go home. Surprise, we were stopping for pizza on the way. Great, more faking it.

As we ate, the boys talked about all the rides and sports as there was a baseball game on the TV in the pizza parlor. Austin's mom asked how my day was. I thanked her multiple times for taking me and letting me experience a city pastime. It was all small talk. Austin only sort of paid attention to me as he talked with his dad, his brothers, and their friends. I was torn between being hurt and being glad.

It was after 10:00 p.m. when I got home. Austin insisted on walking me to the door. He gave me a hug and bid me good night. I thought people would be asleep but they were all up watching a movie. They looked my way, said hi, and asked if I wanted some popcorn. I decided to pass and went down to my room. In spite of how tired I was, I wrote in my journal about the conversation.

> *What do I make of all of this? Could I wait five years for him? What would I do as I waited? Do I go to school or live with my family and do nothing? Doing nothing seems like a waste of valuable time. I am not sure I want to go to college. It seems like a waste of money for a homemaker. Why can I not get a clear simple answer? I wish he had said no now. And what if I do wait and he says no in five years? What would I do?*

My hand cramped and my mind stopped. Clearly it was time to go to bed.

CHAPTER 20

I was able to sleep until eight the next morning. That was a blessing. I was thankful Evalynn was still asleep. I expected her to beg me for details as soon as she woke up. I went upstairs for breakfast and was greeted with Amelia's smile.

"Good morning, Sarai. Did you sleep well?"

"I did, thank you. Did you?"

"Yes, thank you." She put a plate of food together for me. I sat at the counter as no one else was awake yet. I ate a few bites and Amelia pretended to be busy cleaning mixing bowls. I knew she wanted to ask about my date but was containing herself.

When I finished my breakfast, I took my plate into the kitchen and put it in the dishwasher. I looked at Amelia and said, "It was wonderful as always." Amelia smiled. "You may ask if you like." I realized how much I appreciated the self-restraint of those at home.

Amelia's smile widened, thankful for permission. "How is your heart today? Were you able to speak with Austin?"

I looked down. "My heart is more confused than ever. We were able to speak, and he does not have the intention to marry me but he said maybe in five years." I looked at Amelia. "What does it mean? How do you decide with a 'maybe'?" She didn't answer me but shook her head with an "I don't know" look. "I keep asking the questions people say to ask, but it only leads to more confusion."

"Did you receive a response from Matthew?"

"I did." I looked down again.

"What did he say?"

"He wrote to me a response of ten pages explaining everything he believes with references from the Word."

"Why does that sadden you?"

"I know it should not because our hearts are the same. But because of his family, I was expecting something completely different from him. Instead, he asked forgiveness for not sharing his heart or pursuing mine."

"That is a good thing, Sarai." Amelia smiled gently.

I turned away. I was feeling ashamed. "I know it is a good thing. But he is not supposed to be like my father. He is supposed to be cold, uncaring, so I can be done with him and walk away without looking back." The words sounded awful as they came out of my mouth.

Amelia hugged me, and instead of condemning me, she said, "I cannot pretend to understand your feelings as I had very few doubts about marrying Samuel, but is it not better to know exactly who you are walking away from when you do walk away than to find out later you made a mistake. And if you feel the need to look back, is it the right decision?"

I turned around and looked at her. I couldn't tell if she was making sense, so I asked, "Why could Austin not say if he would marry me or not?"

"Here, marriage is not taken as seriously in some ways and people feel they must do certain things or have certain things before they can get married. Perhaps it is better to say it is more of two people in a contract, not a covenant bond where two become one under God's headship."

I looked at her confused. "I do not understand. Why not simply say no?"

Uncle Mark startled us both by saying, "He is a teenaged boy who does not know what he wants. If he says no, he knows he will lose you right now and for now he knows he wants you. If he says yes, well, seventeen-year-old boys in this culture for the most part are afraid of marriage. He is not sure if that is what he wants long term. I am making generalizations, but that is my best guess."

I nodded, still not fully understanding, but would think about what he said. Since no one else was around, I took the opportunity to ask, "Uncle Mark, why did you decide to stay in the city?"

He winced at the question but answered, "I had always wanted to attend university and study medicine. I did not know if I would be allowed to stay long enough to finish medical school, but in my freshman year of university, I met a girl that I wanted to marry. At first she seemed all right with my plans and I thought she wanted to get married. I will add I did not truly know God then. I went home for the summer and broke the news to everyone and they begged me to change my mind, but I would not listen. I was in love and wanted what I wanted. In my junior year, she came to me and said she did not love me and would not put me through medical school. I spent the rest of the year attempting to win her back but to no avail. That summer I went home but was immediately asked to leave. I initially stayed for a woman but was forced to stay because I would not be taken back." It was clearly a painful memory.

"Thank you for telling me this." I went to him and hugged him.

He looked at me in the eyes and said, "Choose wisely, Sarai. I would gladly take you in if needed, but I do not want us to share the hurt that I have."

I nodded. That I did understand.

*****

As predicted, Evalynn grilled me with questions. I kept my answers to her shallow. It was so odd seeing the differences between us and our perceptions of "normal." When she was satisfied I had told her everything that was important, she went upstairs for breakfast.

I was left alone to think and write. I decided to write Matthew and tell him what I believed. Honestly, I wanted to write, "I believe as you do," and be done with it, but God was prompting me to get back in His Word and really seek Him before stating what I believed.

The day was beautiful and so I decided to sit outside in the hammock. I took my Bible and a lot of book marks and I read and marked for hours. I had never dug into the Word like that before, but it was so refreshing. As I read and marked, I began to be able to hear a little better. I remembered the voice at that beach saying, "Pay attention." Right at that moment God had my full, undivided attention. I skipped lunch and read well into the afternoon. By evening I could articulate in detail what I believed and why. I went inside and wrote it down, returning a ten-page letter to Matthew.

I did not come out of the day with a final decision about the future, but I was now focused on God and I was wanting to pay attention to what He said.

The next few days flew by. We did a few fun things but mostly spent time with friends. Tuesday it was time to pack for the youth group mission trip. We were going a couple of states over to help some people who were starting a new church in another big city.

As I was packing up in the afternoon, I received a letter from Mama.

> My sweet Sarai,
>
> I have been praying for you to have peace and clarity. I am sorry you are agonizing and it breaks my heart to hear of it. I cannot tell you who you are, but from what I know of you, you are a child of God who needs to seek first His kingdom and His righteousness. Trust in Jesus and His work in your life. I await your return where I can talk to you face to face.
>
> Much love,
> Mama

The timing was perfect. The verse was where God had been leading my heart during the previous days. It was exactly what I needed to hear. I thought about writing her before the trip but decided to wait until I returned.

CHAPTER 21

We were out of the door at 7:00 a.m. to get breakfast before our long road trip. We were a little early to the church, but a few people were already there. Evalynn and I claimed seats in a van. I decided I wanted to sit on the front row this time. When Mrs. Leland arrived, I asked if she could ride on my van and was so thankful when she said yes.

Austin showed up just before we gathered to pray. I took him to our seats and he asked if we could move back. I told him maybe later, but I wanted to start in the front. He looked disappointed but said it was fine. The group prayed, said goodbye to family, loaded up, and was off.

Once on the interstate, I asked Mrs. Leland, "Why are we going to another city to help with starting a new church? I have seen many churches since leaving my town. I do not understand why you would need more."

Mrs. Leland smiled and responded, "Even with all of the churches we have, there are many who do not know God.

"But why start new churches? Why not just work with the ones that are already meeting?"

"That is a little harder to answer. There are churches that reach out to the community, but some don't. There are also different types of churches that have differences in thought or preferences. But the primary reason for starting churches is to obey Jesus by telling others about Himself, which, hopefully, will bring about new churches as the number of believers grows."

I pondered on this for a minute as it was interesting to me. "Our town only has one church, so the idea of multiple is odd to me. It does sound like it could be a good thing."

"Thank God that your town has a church, because there are many places around the world that do not have churches. They do not know God at all."

"Is that so? How can people not know God?"

"Some people live in places that have different religions that teach about false gods or lies about God. In some countries, people are taught that the rulers and government are gods and they must do what they say or the government doesn't allow religion."

This was perplexing. I looked at Austin, Evalynn, and Amberly. "Do you know about this?" They all nodded. "Does it bother you that there are people who do not know about Jesus?"

They looked at each other with puzzled looks. I was amazed they did not respond with an emphatic "*Yes!*" My heart was breaking.

Evalynn took the role of spokesperson. "It is sad but what can we do? We can't just go or anything."

"Why not?" I asked quite forcefully.

"We're teenagers! We don't have money or jobs or anything. You have to have stuff like that to go."

I looked at all of their faces and then back to Mrs. Leland. "There must be something I can do."

Mrs. Leland smiled. "Pray for those who do not know and share Jesus with everyone you see. That's a good place to begin."

I nodded and thought about this. Evalynn and Amberly talked behind me. Austin put his arm around my shoulders and tried to talk to me about something else but I shook him off. I could not think about anything else. After getting back into my Bible, I knew that people not knowing Jesus and being taught lies was not good and I wanted to know what to do.

*****

The trip was long and I talked little. I thought and prayed but was unable to read or write due to the movement. I listened to the conversations around me as well. It was all shallow, frivolous. Clearly something was going on in my heart more than before.

I was so thankful when we arrived at our hotel twelve hours after leaving the church. I shared a room with Evalynn, Amberly, and Denise. As soon as I got to our room, I put my night clothes on and crashed.

*****

Thankfully I was up with the dawn the next morning so I dressed, grabbed my journal, and went to where they showed us breakfast would be served. It was still being set out when I got there so I sat and wrote about what I had learned during the van ride.

> *I am so thankful the Lord prepared me before this trip. It is different focusing on God and hearing His words. As Mrs. Leland explained the lack of knowledge of Truth in the world, I was heartbroken. To make it worse, my friends seemed so unconcerned. And as I thought on this and my current struggle of where to go, the answer seems so insignificant as I realize God can use me anywhere. People are lost at home and around the world, so now I must ask God where He wants me to be for His work. In some sense the who is second-ary, I suppose, but what do I do if I do not marry?*

I pondered on this for a moment before thinking to myself, "Why does God have to make things so complicated? I want to honor Him, but I still have this real struggle that is right in front of me. I have to marry!" I put my head in my hands. I wanted to hit myself a few times but refrained.

"Breakfast is ready," one of the workers said to me.

I looked at her and replied, "Thank you." I went and got a plate full of food. I was thankful it was "all you could eat." When I returned to the table Mrs. Leland was there.

"Glad to see another early riser!" she said smiling.

"I live on a farm. I wake with the sun regularly." I sat down.

"That makes sense. How are you today?"

I swallowed a bite of egg. "I am challenged and confused."

"How so?"

"Learning the great need of Jesus in the world is challenging me. I am still confused about who to marry." I explained to her the conversation with Austin and the letter from Matthew as well as my extensive search into the Scripture. I shared my journal entry and the thoughts that followed. I concluded with, "Why can God not stand in front of me and say 'This is what I want you to do'?"

Mrs. Leland placed her hand on mine. "It would be nice if He did that wouldn't it? I have asked that question before. But as I have grown in Christ I have come to understand that that's just not how God works. Mark 12:30 and 31 say, 'You shall love the Lord, your God, with all of your heart, and with all of your soul, and with all of your mind and with all of your strength' and 'You shall love your neighbor as yourself.' Our call is to love Him as He has loved us first and then to love others as He has loved us, so begin there. Are you loving God with all of your heart, soul, mind, and strength?"

I thought about this. "I am not sure. After my time in the Word this weekend past, I would say I am now more than I was. I now want to love Him."

"That's great. So how do these things you want show your love for God?"

That was a tough question. "I suppose the desire to share Jesus is one way to love God, because that is what the Bible says. I do not know how marriage fits into love for God."

"Marriage is a picture of Christ and the church. But the Bible does not require us to be married. Look at Paul: He served God faithfully and wrote a lot of the New Testament but was never married. But God also uses marriage to conform us to Christ's likeness. Look here in Ephesians 5, starting in verse 22. It says, "Wives, be subject to your own husbands as to the Lord. For the husband is the head of the wife, as Christ also is the head of the church, He Himself being the Savior of the body. But as the church is subject to Christ, so also the wives ought to be to their husbands in everything. Husbands, love your wives, just as Christ loved the church and gave Himself up for her, so that He might sanctify her, having cleansed her by the washing of water with the word, that He might present to Himself the church in all her glory, having no spot or wrinkle or any such thing; but that she would be holy and blameless." The question is not do you get married but goes back to what I told you at camp. Will you be better for God's kingdom together or apart? Will you model Christ and the church? The other question to ask yourself is do you love God more than the man?"

The last question pierced through the heart quite a lot. I began thinking about my response to Austin since I had been in the city. The truth was I had wanted Austin more than God. On the other hand, I had not wanted Matthew at all. How should I reconcile this?

"Are you telling me I should not marry Austin, because I have been putting him above God?"

"Not necessarily. We are sinners who get things mixed up sometimes, but I would consider why that happened and if your attraction was more self-glorifying or God-glorifying."

"My other question is should I marry Matthew if I do not love him?"

"Again I would say not necessarily. Why don't you love him?"

"I believe I explained a little at camp about his family and that we have nothing in common. I also do not desire him."

"But none of that has to do with love."

Questions filled my face. "I do not understand."

"Look here at Romans 5:8: 'But God demonstrates His own love toward us, in that while we were yet sinners, Christ died for us.' God's love for those who hated Him allowed Him to send is Son to die for us. That is the greatest love of all. In 1 Corinthians 13, we are told that love is patient, kind, not jealous, is not arrogant or boastful, seeks others best interest, rejoices in truth, bears, believes, endures, and hopes all things. It never fails. So you see love is not merely a feeling but a choice in how we choose to treat others and how we think of them. I would say, generally speaking, that feeling of love and admiration will follow as we obey God's commands. It is not a guarantee, but it is very likely. Our standard is to love God above all and love your neighbor as yourself. Think of these things in light of how you view and treat others, especially when choosing to marry."

In all my study in the Bible, I had not thought about marriage and other relationships. It was eye opening. "I certainly must reflect on this more. Thank you for pointing me to God's Word and not merely your own ideas."

"You're welcome. That's what we're to do. Only God can tell you what's best for you. I do want to encourage you to not look so much at the surface of these two boys, but look deep, as deep as you possibly can, to truly see who they are. Ask God to reveal their hearts to you. In fact, didn't you just tell me that Matthew sent you a ten-page letter explaining his beliefs?"

I nodded. A group of middle school girls came to breakfast and we ended the deep conversation, but I couldn't help but think, maybe we have more in common than I think. Mrs. Leland went to get a plate. I prayed in my head, "Lord, please help me see their hearts. I need to know who they really are." I thought about the conversations with Austin and the letters that Matthew had sent and tried to see them as God would.

As I got another plate of food, Austin came in. "Good morning, beautiful." He gave me a side hug.

I smiled slightly. "Good morning." I felt some butterflies in my stomach. What was that about?

"This breakfast looks great!" Austin piled his plate as full as he could. He sat down next to me. "Looking forward to today?"

"Yes. I am excited to learn about this city and how one may go about beginning a new church."

"Yeah, that's cool. I'm hoping to play some basketball in the park."

Internally I rolled my eyes. We talked about our expectations for the week, and I began to realize how different we really are from each other.

People continued to trickle in, many in pajamas, which I found quite odd and a little disturbing. Evalynn and Amberly joined us talking about their hopes for the week, mostly the free times we would have.

At 8:00 a.m., we all gathered in the lobby and loaded into the vans to drive to the house of the family that was starting the church. It was a small tasteful home in a crowded area of the city. There wasn't much room, but we squished into the living room to meet Pastor Jackson and his family. He gave us a few more details about our projects for the week before assigning groups to go to a few parks in the area to meet people and invite them to camps we would be having the next week.

Amazingly I ended up in a group with both Evalynn and Austin and thankfully the Lelands were one set of adult leaders. Our group loaded into its van and headed on. The park was beautiful for the crowded setting around it. There was a walking track around the whole thing. On one end was a children's playground, swings, tables and benches, and an area where you could spray water on each other. The other side had an area marked off for football or soccer and a basketball court. The boys grabbed a basketball and took off for the court. I saw kids swinging and went to join them.

I sat next to a girl of about five and tried to talk to her. She was shy and went to her mother. I smiled and waved to the mom, but she turned and walked away. I thought it strange but reminded myself that people in the city were not always comfortable talking to people they don't know. I kept swinging and looked for another opportunity.

A couple of older kids came to swing, and they talked back but ignored me before I could tell them about the camps in the park the following week. No one had warned us this would be difficult.

A mom with a toddler came a little later, so I slowed to talk to her. She was a little responsive and I told her about the camp. She was interested but did not know about bringing such a little one. I wanted to invite her to the Sunday meeting but did not know where or what time it was.

I went to ask Mrs. Leland for the information, but the woman was gone when I came back. I went back to Mrs. Leland to find out why people were so reluctant to talk to me. She explained that often people do not trust strangers and some are shy. She encouraged me to walk around and keep trying. So I did. There were not many people when we first arrived, but as the morning went on it began to fill. By eleven, the boys had drawn many kids from the neighborhood and had a full basketball game going. This afforded some opportunities to some of the neighborhood girls who had come to watch. We talked to them about the area and told them we would have camps in the park, giving them flyers to take home about it.

Around noon, the pastors brought a lot of pizza for us and to share with the kids. That was pretty neat. The pizza was gone in no time and most of the soda too. The men led a short devotional while we finished eating and told everyone about our camp the next week.

When we finished eating, the boys went back to basketball and the girls to the sidelines. I talked some but mostly listened to the things the girls were saying. Much of it I did not understand, but when I could, it sounded very different and, in many ways, sad.

At three, we said goodbye to the kids and loaded up to go to Pastor Jackson's house. When we arrived only one other group was already present. We sat in the living room chatting and waiting. Austin sat next to me and put his arm around my shoulders, but he turned to talk to one of the guys from the other group. I tried to shrug it off as I listened to Amberly and Evalynn next to me. They talked about swimming in the hotel pool that evening and asked if I would come. I agreed, though I didn't want to. Austin still did not look my way when I talked. I know I was not talking to him, but I thought he might turn if he heard me talking about swimming.

Seriously, what was wrong with me? Because of where I grew up, I knew men were not always where you were and that they did not pay attention to you every second they were in your presence, but for some reason, a day of being right next to him and his giving me attention without giving me attention was upsetting me. What did that mean? Nothing in the Scriptures Mrs. Leland had shared with me pointed directly to that problem.

The other two groups arrived and we talked about the day. Mostly people talked about the games they had played or just hung out. I debated about sharing the struggle of people responding to conversation but decided to keep quiet. Clearly everyone else had had a fun day and I did not want to rain on it. The next day was a play day and we would be going to a local amusement park with both dry and water rides. The group was very excited. I wondered why we were wasting a day of work, but again kept quiet.

Pastor Vaughn prayed for our dinner, and we went to the back-yard for a cookout. There was so much food and we all ate a lot.

After dinner, we went back to the hotel for free time, and we headed to the pool. It was a smaller indoor pool so it got crowded very quickly. I decided to sit on the edge with my feet in the water. My friends tried to coax me in, but the crowd with the boys rough housing was too much for me. Needing my bathing suit the next day for the park made me stand all the more firm.

I decided to head to our room earlier than the others, so I could have a few minutes to journal and pray alone before bed. I tried to process what I was thinking and feeling about Austin but had a difficult time. What was I really thinking? What was I really feeling? I wrote about the day and read over it. "Pay attention." The voice resonated in my head. *To what am I paying attention?* I thought. No response. I began to reread when the other girls came in. I closed my journal and put it away. I listened to their chatter as I laid down and allowed it to lull me to sleep.

CHAPTER 22

The amusement park was fun. I enjoyed trying the water slides and really preferred the wet rides to the dry. Unfortunately we had to stay in groups so I went all over. Austin acted more like he had when we went to the park together which was nice. We talked here and there, but I had nothing serious to talk about and that was kind of odd. Was I having fun?

Upon returning to the hotel, I did not go to the pool but went straight to our room. I wrote about the day and wondered,

> *Is it a bad thing that I am only happy with Austin when he is with me and giving me attention? Is that my expectation of him? How do I handle this? Is this love like I believed that it was? I am more confused now than I have ever been, and I do not know what to do.*

I wanted to cry but refrained in case the other girls came back. I pulled out my Bible. I looked back at some of the verses that Mrs. Leland had showed me. I wrote in my journal the verses on love and wrote my thoughts on them and what that might look like.

Then the question came to my mind, "Does Austin really love me?" I looked back at the verse and my notes. "Maybe." And then the next obvious question, "Does Matthew really love me?" I reviewed the verses again. "I think he might." I thought back to his letters;

his in-depth answer to my untraditional question, his release of me, his kind words when I was accused. I could no longer hold back the tears. "No! This is not how it is supposed to be. I am not to feel this way! What is wrong with me? What is happening?"

I closed my journal and hid under the covers. At least I could hide my tears. I heard the others come in and pretended to be asleep. They tried to be quiet but failed and so I fell asleep to the conversation around me.

I woke up with the sun on Saturday. After dressing, I took my Bible and journal and went to the breakfast area. I read and meditated on a few of the verses on love again while the workers put out breakfast. As soon as it was ready, I ate and then went to walk around outside the hotel. I prayed for peace and clarity and to be able to focus on God throughout the day.

At 9:00 a.m., we loaded up and went to Pastor Jackson's house. The plan for the day was to hand out flyers around our designated parks about the camps next week. I had a little twinge of nervousness but was excited to talk to as many people as possible. We went to our parks with neighborhood maps and divided into groups of four. I was with Austin, Evalynn, and Mrs. Leland. Mrs. Leland asked who wanted to go first and I volunteered. We rehearsed what we were to say and went to the first house. No answer. It took five houses for someone to answer the door. I gave them the flyer and told them the information. Mrs. Leland did the next house. Both Austin and Evalynn asked not to. They were afraid.

Austin is a coward, I thought. *If he will not share about these camps what else will he not share?* I was blown away and paying close attention. *Matthew would knock on these doors with you and speak for the camps.* My stomach tightened. What was I thinking? Was this true?

Mrs. Leland asked each of them to do one house a piece, but she and I spoke at the rest of the houses.

Lunch was at Pastor Jackson's house. His wife had made lasagna for us. It smelled amazing. I ate outside with Austin, Evalynn, and Amberly who talked about swimming again. Why did they talk about swimming and free time so much? But that was not my most pressing question. I turned to Austin and asked, "Why would you not knock on doors today?"

Austin squirmed a little. Clearly I had hit a nerve. "I don't like going to talk to people I don't know."

I was confused. "I do not understand that from you. You came to me and pursued me without knowing me. What is the difference?"

"I didn't knock on a random door and you happen to be there."

"So you speak to everyone that you do not know at church?" I felt like I was scolding him, but I really did not understand.

"Well, no." Austin stammered over the words.

"Then why talk to me if you are uncomfortable talking to people that you do not know."

He squirmed more, clearly not wanting to answer.

"Well?" I did my best to hold my temper.

"You're pretty," he finally admitted, blushing. The truth was finally out in the open.

We sat in silence for a couple of minutes. I debated over what to ask next. "How do you expect to be involved in God's ministry if you cannot talk to people that you do not know?" I asked calmly.

At this, he was the one who looked confused. "I'm not going into the ministry. That's what pastors and missionaries do. I don't have to do that as a pharmacist or something. People will be coming to me."

I realized then he had no intention of being involved in lay church ministry. He was focused on his ideas and plans and not God's. My eyes were being quickly opened.

"I see." I had nothing else to say.

Austin did have something to add, however. "Why are you so focused on this? We're still teens. Loosen up and relax so we can have fun."

I thought about this. I only had a couple of weeks left in the city before returning home. Can I simply ignore God's general call and only have fun? I did not know the answer so I said, "I will think on it." I did want to have fun, but when I had such heavy decisions on my mind, it made it challenging.

We had the afternoon free. I decided to go swimming and try to have fun like everyone else. I thought, *If I could just make a decision then I can 'let loose and relax,' but I do not feel like I have enough facts to make a decision.*

Mrs. Leland came in shortly after so I asked her, "How do you have fun when you have a big decision weighing on your mind?"

"I tell myself I'll think about it later and focus on what I'm doing at the moment. Having some fun can help relax you so you can better think about it later."

That sounded like a plan to me. I did just that and thought about playing around. I tried my best to play with my friends as I had before and did all right with it.

*****

Sunday morning's sermon was about love, ironically enough, and how God's love should fill us and pour out of us. It really reiterated many of the things Mrs. Leland had told me and reflected what I had been recording in my journal. I was not completely sure what God was telling me long term in this, but I felt certain that He would make it clear.

*****

The week was a pretty typical kid's camp week. There ended up being about forty kids from the neighborhood and we did crafts, told Bible stories, played games, ate snacks, and had fun with the kids. Mr. Leland did share about salvation in Christ every day, which I found amazing. A few of the kids responded with questions and a couple seemed to genuinely believe in Christ's work for them. It was really neat to see.

Friday night, we had a cookout in the park for the kids who attended and their families. So many people came, including others from the neighborhood who happened to be walking by. So many of the mothers I met were raising their kids alone, which broke my heart. There was so much need and nothing I could do. When I could, I shared the story of Jesus and what God had done in my life. A couple were interested but most only listened politely and then changed the subject.

As people finished eating, Mr. Leland shared a Bible story with a message of the saving knowledge of Christ. He invited people with questions to talk with us and told them about church on Sunday.

Afterward, the guys started a basketball game. I went to talk with more moms. I was interested to hear some of their stories and grow in my understanding of people. I did not realize how much heartache was in the world. I did not know that families could completely fall apart without knowing what happened. What had happened to my family was hard, but it was nothing compared to what these people had lived through. Part of me wanted to stay here and help, but I needed more education or training before I tackled something like that.

I enjoyed the evening. We went back to Pastor Jackson's house to talk about our cookouts and debrief the week. One group said they had fifteen people accept Christ that night. I wish I could have seen that. We spent some time praying for the city and Pastor Jackson and his family and the spread of the Gospel there. It was nice. We received instructions for the morning as we would be heading back to my cousin's home city and said goodbye to the Jackson family. I was a little sad but thankful for time to process this experience before going to my home. God was clearly opening me up to something.

*****

We left the hotel parking lot at 8:00 a.m. sharp. Everyone was tired and trying to sleep on the vans. I agreed to sit with Austin on the second row. He told me I could lie on his shoulder if I wanted to rest and put his arm around me.

"No, thank you, Austin. I am not really tired. I usually get up before dawn."

"That's so weird. Why do you do that?"

"I live on a farm, and we must awaken early to accomplish all of our tasks. We cook on fire and from scratch always. It takes more time to do what we must."

"But you're on vacation. You can sleep more. Do it!" He tried to pull me down on his shoulder.

I pulled back and looked him in the eyes. "I am not tired, Austin. I do not wish to sleep."

"Okay, sorry. I just thought you'd like to rest while you can." He looked annoyed.

"Thank you, but I would prefer to look out the window and enjoy the view."

"Fine," he huffed, pulled me as close as he could, and looked out the window.

It was then that I realized how much he had been holding on to me physically. We had not talked much, but when we were sitting together, he almost always had his arm around me or was holding my hand. That was weird. Why was he doing that, but not really getting to know me more?

The drive was long once again. After lunch, people began to talk more or sing. I mostly listened and tried to pay attention to what Austin was doing. He was rubbing my arm and getting as close as possible to me. I didn't say anything, but it felt odd. Something was not quite right.

CHAPTER 23

Sunday began our last week in the city. After church, I wrote about thoughts and ideas I had had during the mission trip. I thought about what my long-term decision should be. I processed the last three months to the best of my ability. I still had questions and decided to wait to see what was at home before I made a long-term decision.

Monday was very low key. I talked with Aunt Dianna about some of the things I had heard.

"How can papas leave their babies with no care for them?" That was something I could not wrap my mind around.

Aunt Dianna smiled. "Mark told me y'all were sheltered from so much. This world is broken, Sarai, and people are selfish. Some men don't even know they have babies because they do what they want with whomever they want and do not think of the consequences or whom they might hurt. It's not a great answer, but ultimately it goes back to the sinfulness of man."

"That is very sad."

"Yes."

"What can I do to help them?"

"Pray for them. If you ever come back to the city, invest in the lives of these kids. They need Jesus. God is the best Father, and through Jesus, they can have a Father."

I nodded.

When the mail came, I had a letter from Matthew.

My dearest Sarai,

Thank you so much for your letter telling me your heart. It is more beautiful than I thought, and I am grateful to know you more. I want to know even more about you. What are your passions, your desires? What do you like? What do you dislike? What have you experienced in the city? What is God teaching you now?

I realize this is a lot and that you might not have time to write before you return. If you do not, I look forward to discussing these things with you when I can look into your beautiful eyes. I also look forward to hearing more of what you have learned and experienced during your time in the city. I await your return, my darling, Sarai.

Your beloved,
Matthew

My eyes were moist. "He wants to know me more? He thinks my heart and my eyes are beautiful?" This was far more than I expected. Did I really know Matthew? I had been judging someone I did not know.

I decided to write him a letter, but instead of sending it, I planned to keep it and read it to him. I thought about these things so I could write coherently. In some ways, the answers to the questions were changing, so I wanted to write what I knew for sure and then tackle the newer passions and interests that were forming. I worked on it all evening and was satisfied with another ten-page letter for Matthew.

*****

The rest of the week was spent in various summer activities. Late Friday afternoon, we all loaded up for a picnic in the park. When we arrived, there were a lot of people from my uncle's church to give me a going-away party. I was so touched. There was a lot of food, some of which I still had not experienced in the city. I talked to people and ate. They gave me cards and gifts to remember my visit, as if I would be able to forget. A few people shared kind words and stories. It was sweet. Finally Evalynn gave me a book with pictures and notes in it. It was amazing! We had nothing like this at home, and I was excited to show Papa and Mama. They closed the presentation with a time of prayer for me. The tears flowed. Afterward, we ate cake and ice cream. So good!

When the formal party was finished, Austin said to me, "Can we walk by the creek?"

"I can do that," I replied with a smile.

Austin held out his hand to me. I hesitated but decided to take it. He led me away from the crowd and to a more quiet area of the park where a slow trickling brook rolled by. "It's been a fun summer. I'm so glad I met you, Sarai." He turned to look at me. "You are so beautiful." He grabbed my other hand and gazed deep into my eyes. I didn't know what to say or what to think. "I'm sorry it's taken me so long to do this." Austin leaned in, and before I knew it, his face was right next to mine.

The moment his lips touched mine I jumped back and looked at him. "What are you doing?"

His face had as much confusion as mine did. "Giving you a kiss."

"Why would you do that?"

"Because I like you, we've been going out this summer. You're going away for a while."

"You are making the assumption that I will be coming back. You say you like me and we have been together this summer, but yet you will not commit to me. Why, then, do you believe you can kiss me?"

He clearly did not understand. "What is your problem, Sarai? This is how relationships progress and move forward."

"This maybe how relationships progress here, but not from where I come. We talk to each other. We get to know each other's families and see our betrothed interact with others." My mind went to my times with Matthew and watching him. I compared it to my three months with Austin. They were far more different than I had previously realized.

Austin interrupted my thoughts. "We've been doing that. And why should I not assume you're coming back. From everything you've said, I know you want to be here."

"Perhaps there is a part of me that does, but to what end? I have no guarantee from you, and God may not want me here."

"Why would you say that? You said you want out of your town. If God gave you that desire, surely He wants you here. And even if we don't end up married, you can find someone else."

I couldn't take anymore. My heart was completely shattered. "How dare you! You pretend you care for me, but you do not care for me at all. Do you have any idea how much my heart is aching right now? Why would you hurt someone you like?" I felt the tears coming.

"I had no idea I hurt you, Sarai." He reached for my cheek but I moved back and turned. "Sarai."

"No, please do not do this. You have made yourself clear." I turned and walked back toward the group.

Austin caught me halfway and turned me around. "Sarai, I don't want us to just end. It could still work between us."

"I do not know if I can trust you. You have completely dismissed God in this conversation. You assume my desire is from God. Right now I am unsure where God wants me, and I need to seek Him first. If it were to work between us a great deal would have to change, and I am not sure I can wait around for five years hoping you might change. Goodbye, Austin."

I turned and walked back to the party. I was done and I did not look back.

Saturday morning was bittersweet. I was almost thankful for the previous evening, as I had no current reason to stay. Evalynn was up early with me. I packed and she asked me about my thoughts of returning in the future.

"I hope I will return for a visit. As for moving here, I am not yet sure. I think I know my decision, but I must go home and see with my new eyes what is there. Then I must pray."

"I think I get it, but I don't know why you'd want to stay in a place that rejects family for being different."

"I am not saying I want to be there, but I am open to God using me where ever He takes me."

She nodded. I'm not sure she understood. I turned and hugged her. This time she was the one with tears. It did not take long for me to join her in a light cry. She hugged me back. "Don't forget us, please."

Releasing her, I looked into Evalynn's eyes. "I will *never* forget you, Evalynn. I will not be able. You are my cousin, and I love you."

"I love you too, Sarai." She embraced me again. "I hate not knowing my family."

"I will write you as often as I am able, and tell you how our family is and write you about those you may never meet."

"Thank you, Sarai. That would be great."

"Let us pray that God will open the hearts of those in my town so you may meet them one day."

Evalynn nodded, and I prayed.

Then I said, "Now I must get my things together and get dressed to go. Samuel will be ill if I am not ready on time." I checked my duffle and pulled out my clothes to wear home. "I cannot take the wonderful clothes you bought with me. They would not be allowed. You wear them."

Shaking her head, Evalynn said, "They will stay in your drawer until you come back to wear them."

We both smiled. I donned my home clothes, pulled my hair back in a tight bun, and put on my scarf. *It is time to go home,* I thought as I looked in the mirror. Though I looked like the Sarai that came to the city, a new Sarai was going home. I liked the new Sarai far better.

CHAPTER 24

Samuel packed the car and all of the women hugged and cried. Uncle Mark got us all together for one last photo before we left. One more round of hugs and thank-yous, and we got in the car and drove away.

We were silent for quite a while. I watched the familiar scenes roll by the window until we got on the interstate. I sighed.

"Are you doing all right, Sarai?" Amelia asked.

My eyes started to water a little. "I am, thank you."

"What are you thinking?"

What was I thinking? A little of this and a little of that. "Many things are in my mind right now. I am sad to be leaving our family knowing there is a possibility I may never see them again. I am happy to be going home, and I did not think I would be. I am thankful that I had this time in a different environment to learn and grow. At the same time I almost wish I did not know life could be different. It is all a mess."

I saw Amelia nod. "We understand that quite well."

Samuel then said, "Have you made your decision about where to be come May."

That was more abrupt than I expected. "No, I have not yet. I want to see how it is at home before making such a heavy decision. I do not wish to cause any unnecessary burdens."

Samuel smiled. "You have certainly gained some wisdom."

It was my turn to smile. Had I gained wisdom? In growing closer to God, I guess I had. I remembered what Amelia said a couple of minutes earlier and asked, "Amelia, you said that you understand my thought. Do you think of staying in the city?"

Samuel responded. "We are also torn between the two lifestyles. There are many things we like about the city, but our purpose is clear for now, we are to learn about modern tools to see if we can use this new technology at home. I plan to finish next summer and come home to live."

I had nothing to say to that. His life was clear. Even I could see that. *Lord, make my life that clear,* I prayed in my mind.

We drove farther and farther away from the city. More trees, the start of some pasture land. I began to get butterflies. I was nervous, but why? Was I nervous to be back home? Was I nervous to see people from home? Was I nervous to see Matthew? Probably all of the above.

Before I knew it, the modern town was visible in the distance. My heart pounded as the butterflies grew. A few minutes later, we were pulling into the bus station parking lot, and there was Papa waiting for us in the wagon. As soon as the car stopped, I opened the door and ran to Papa. He was already half way to me. "Papa!" I jumped into his arms. He swung me around like I was a little girl.

"My precious, Sarai," he said with excitement and kissed my forehead. "How I have missed you." He set me down with a huge smile. "The whole family is waiting to see you."

"Even Josiah?" my voice was hopeful.

Papa put his hand on my shoulder. "He is happy you are home."

I nodded. Samuel came up with the bigger bags and greeted Papa briefly before putting them in the wagon. I went to grab my purse and get in the wagon. I had forgotten how nice the feel of wood was. It was the first reminder that I was really back home. Samuel and Amelia settled and we were off. The horses trotted at a mild pace. The wagon bounced rhythmically beneath us. My heart began to quicken again as we rolled toward familiar ground. The first of the houses and fields came into view. My heart beat faster. I saw people. Did I dare wave? I kept my decorum instead of causing an immediate stir.

Our house came into view and a smile spread across my face. Mama and the kids were standing out front anxiously waiting for us. I could not hold it in any longer. I waved as hard as I could and saw them wave back. Mama had to keep the little ones from running to us on the road. I wanted Papa to make the horses gallop but knew he would not.

As soon as we stopped in front of the house, I jumped down and went straight to Mama. We embraced so tightly I could barely breathe. My eyes began to water. "I missed you so much, Mama."

"I missed you, also my sweet." She squeezed me even tighter. Finally she looked at me with a loosened embrace. "You look more grown up and peaceful."

I smiled at Mama. "It was a good summer."

Mama nodded. "I look forward to hearing more about your trip."

She released me and I hugged the little ones. Magdalene had gotten so big. Tamar was thankful to have me back to help in the kitchen. Josiah greeted me coldly. "I am glad you made the best choice." I simply nodded. I wanted to yell at him but remained calm and went back to Mama. She instructed me to get my purse and come in for dinner. I was not about it argue. Amelia was a great cook, but I was ready for Mama's fire cooked cuisine.

I picked up my things and walked quickly toward the house. I opened the door and stopped immediately. There was everyone who had come to bid us farewell. Standing in the front was Matthew, beaming from ear to ear. I smiled back and blushed. I wanted to hug him, but instead I walked slowly to him.

"Hello, Matthew." My heart raced.

"Hello, Sarai. I am so thankful you are home."

I nodded. "I am as well." I lingered for a moment in front of him before he moved so I could greet the rest of my guests. I looked for Joanna but could not find her. After some of the men left to move the tables outside, I saw her sitting in one of our rockers. I went to her as quickly as I could through the remaining people.

"Joanna!" She was looking out of the window. Clearly she had been crying. "What is wrong?"

She looked at me slowly as I kneeled next to her. "I am so glad you came back to us." She leaned over and embraced me. "I have been so afraid I would lose you forever." And the tears flowed from both of us.

A few minutes later, the dinner bell rang. "Come, Joanna," I said wiping my eyes. "Let us eat. I am famished and I want some of my Mama's food." She smiled and we walked arm and arm outside.

Once all were gathered, Papa blessed the meal and we got our food. I went to the typical girls' table. I was very quickly swarmed by my cousins with all of their new little ones. "Tell us what the city is like." "How do they dress?" "What are the cars like?" "What kind of buildings are there?" "What are the people like?" All the questions came at once. My head was swimming.

"Please, one question at a time." I finally had to say.

They each took turns asking what they wanted to know. I did my best to answer, but there are some things that you cannot explain well to people who have known nothing but farming and simple life. When I was asked about the people, I got a twinge in my stomach. I so desired to tell them about Uncle Mark, Aunt Dianna, and our cousins and how wonderful they were, but I did not know if that would really be wise for us. I simply had to describe them as people we met here and there. I also could not tell them about the trips I took, or what I learned about dating. It was such an incomplete picture of my time, and it made me sad that I could not share it freely.

As I talked with my cousins, I caught myself stealing glances of Matthew and my heart fluttering. It reminded me of when I first met Austin and caused me to think that maybe, just maybe, I still was attracted to Matthew.

People began to leave as the sun started to set. In most ways, nothing had changed. Our people looked the same, talked the same, dressed the same, and celebrated the same. My being gone had made no difference in the way life functioned. It was a bit refreshing to know that life does go on in spite of where I am. Before his family left, Matthew came to me and said, "I wish we could have talked more this evening, but your parents have given me permission to join you for supper tomorrow after church. I look forward to seeing you in the morning."

I smiled at him. "I will see you tomorrow." I started to reach my hand out but quickly caught myself. "Good night." I bowed my head.

"Good night." I watched him walk away with his family. Matthew took his smallest brother and put him on his shoulders. His brother giggled. That sounded like music to my ears. I realized I had not really watched Matthew the last couple of years. I only saw what I wanted to see. Matthew was definitely someone I could marry.

*****

Though I was exhausted, Papa and Mama gave me permission to stay up and talk with them for a little while alone before the morning. We sat in the living room after my brothers and sisters were tucked in. Papa said, "Mama and I wanted a few minutes to talk with you about what you have learned and what is currently in your heart and mind."

Where did I begin? "I learned much this summer, Papa. I learned far more than I expected." I told them about some of my time with Austin and the thoughts and feelings I had dealt with during my time in the city. I told them about my time in the Word and my investigation on Biblical love and marriage. I concluded, "I am still not completely certain of my long-term decision, but I believe spending the afternoon talking with Matthew tomorrow will help."

My parents listened so well and were encouraging as well as sympathetic throughout. Both smiled as I finished talking. "You have, indeed, learned much," Papa said. "I am thankful for the growth God has granted you, even in the pain."

I nodded. "I understand now why you arrange us." I looked at my hands. A couple of tears ran down my cheeks.

Mama lifted my chin. "We know this is not easy for most. We have all learned to accept it without questions, but we wanted you to have the opportunity to know for certain where God would have you. This was the best way."

"I am so grateful for you giving me this opportunity, even with the pain. I only regret that because of my determination I now have a piece of Austin with me forever. He will always be there."

Papa is the one who responded. "We will pray for healing for your heart as you move forward. Know that Matthew is an understanding man and he will also help you to heal if you will allow." I nodded. Papa continued. "Though it is not the conventional courting routine, we have arranged with Mr. and Mrs. March for Matthew to join our family three evenings a week so that you can really know each other and make a fully knowledgeable decision."

"I do not understand, Papa. What does that mean?"

"We want you to have enough meetings so that you can be sure you are to marry Matthew before your chosen day."

"Matthew has agreed to this as well?" My eyes began to tear again.

"Yes, he has. He desires God's best for you, even if it is not him."

He loves me. The tears flowed.

Mama hugged me. "You should get some sleep. Tomorrow is going to be a great day."

I kissed Papa and walked upstairs with Mama. She tucked me in my bed and said, "You know where God is leading. Trust Him." She kissed my forehead. "Good night, Sarai."

"Good night, Mama." In moments, I was asleep.

CHAPTER 25

Dawn awoke me in spite of my fatigue. I thought and prayed for a minute before getting out of bed. "Lord, show me today where you want me. Show me how to love who I need to love." I thought about what I was going to tell Matthew and got my letter, journal, and photo album together so I would not have to rummage for them when he was at the house. I put my house coat on and went to resume my place in my home. It felt good.

Mama told me not to worry but my vacation had been long enough and I was ready to get back to what I knew as normal life. I went outside to collect eggs. There were new baby chicks running around in the coup. I took the eggs to the kitchen and began to scramble them. It was wonderful to be with Mama and Tamar cooking over fire. Yes, it took longer, it was more work, but it was worth it.

Breakfast was delicious. We all put on our Sunday clothes and walked to the town church. It was different from the summer, but it was a pleasure to walk. At church, my family sat together. The March family also sat together across the aisle and a little in front of us. My mind went to the city. I could not concentrate. Everything was the same as when I left, but so different from the summer. It was going to take time to actually readjust to life at home. I had missed home, but three months is enough time to learn new patterns. It was a good reminder also of differences being good.

We walked toward home with the March family until the road split. At that point, Matthew came with us. He and Samuel talked

136

until we arrived at our house. Samuel and Amelia were also joining us for Sunday dinner. It was nice being in our full house.

After eating, Mama dismissed me from dishes to go to the courting table with Matthew. We walked side by side to the back of the room and sat across from each other. Our eyes met and we both smiled. I did not know what to say or where to begin.

An awkward moment passed before Matthew cleared his throat and said, "I know we have many things to discuss and I am certain you have much to share from your time away, but before we decide where to begin, I would like to pray for our conversation."

My smile grew. "I would like that very much." Again I started to reach for his hand but caught myself and shoved my hands in my lap. Matthew prayed a beautiful heartfelt prayer for us as we really learned about each other and sought God's best for us. This was not the Matthew I had left; he had changed much as well.

Matthew said "Amen" then looked back into my eyes and said, "I want to thank you again for not following our ways and asking me about my faith. This helped me to really seek what I believe and showed me where I was lacking in leadership. I still have much to learn about leading a family." I nodded at him. "Thank you also for your response. I knew you were a beautiful young woman, but to hear your heart was so precious." I was floored. It was one thing to write these words to someone in our town, but to say them aloud was unthinkable. "If it is all right with you, I would enjoy hearing your thoughts on the last letter I sent."

"I would be glad to share those things with you. I wrote a response to read to you, but it is upstairs. Please excuse me for just a moment."

Matthew nodded and stood as I did. I walked quickly to my room and picked up the letter. I debated about taking the two books as well but decided to leave them for now. We were clearly going to be given a lot of time together in the next nine months.

Matthew was waiting patiently for me to return and stood when I came downstairs. We sat and I opened the ten pieces of paper and began to read. He listened intently. Occasionally I would stop to see if he had any questions, but we would quickly move forward. He wanted to hear all I had to say.

When I finished, I said, "That is all for right now. I have not thought of anything to add."

"Amazing. You really are an amazing woman." As he said this, I thought I saw his arm twitch as if he wanted to take my hand, but I could have been seeing things.

I blushed at his complement. "Thank you." I looked back to his eyes. "How would you answer these questions, Matthew?"

It was his turn to speak and my turn to listen intently. I was surprised at what I heard. In some ways, we were not so different, especially in our renewed passion for the Lord and His Word. Some things were not so surprising as it was a reflection of our culture, but he was clearly open to seeing the outside world as God would allow. There was now some connection between us beyond the betrothal arrangement our parents made.

This conversation had taken more time than I had realized. Mama, Amelia, and Tamar were already back in the kitchen preparing dinner. "I should go and help with dinner," I said standing.

Matthew stood and said, "Of course."

I went to the kitchen and Matthew to sit with Papa and Samuel. I began working on the biscuits. Mama tried to dismiss me, but I could not let my work go again. I needed a little brain break anyway to process what I had just learned. I loved being in the kitchen hearing Mama talk as we worked. I kind of listened but mostly replayed Matthew's and my conversation in my head. I found myself smiling wider as I thought about it and the possibilities that could come from a union with him.

After dinner, Matthew and I were excused to the courting table again. We sat and Matthew said, "What would you like to discuss now?"

I shrugged slightly, "I do not know. So much has happened it will take some time to tell you all that took place. Perhaps the better question is what do you wish for me to tell you?"

Matthew thought about this for a minute before answering, "Please tell me more about your family."

I was quite pleased with this request. "I would be happy to tell you about them. They are such wonderful people and miss not being able to know our family here." I proceeded to describe each person and some of the things we did together. I concluded with, "They are so generous and loving and it breaks my heart that they cannot come home because of our traditions."

Matthew nodded at this. "I understand your frustration."

This took me aback, "You do?" my face was full of questions. "How can you understand?"

Before he answered, he was able to get Papa's attention and he took the little ones outside. "I apologize, but we need as much privacy as possible to discuss this." He took a deep breath, looked around one more time, and then spoke, "This is a bit challenging to tell, but as we are being honest about all things, I want you to know more about how and why our arrangement took place. Both my parents and your parents have given me permission to share this with you. When your Uncle Mark was refused coming back to our town, your parents were very distraught and desired to keep in contact with him but needed help to do that. Our Papas are best friends as you are well aware and your Papa went to mine in confidence to ask for help. Papa sympathized and agreed. Mama was afraid but Papa told her they should. They were able to get a box at the post office and establish contact in a way that no one else knew. I found out a year ago when I asked why I was having to wait to marry that because of the help my parents offered to yours my parents desired that their oldest son be betrothed to your parents' oldest daughter." He stopped there.

I sat for a moment, thinking about what Matthew had just told me. What was I to make of this? "Our betrothal, then, is a form of repayment to your family?"

"It sounds horrible when you say that, but I think it as much preserving the family secret as it is repayment as you say."

In some way that made sense, but I wasn't sure I liked the thought of being a repayment for help. Maybe that was why Papa and Mama wanted me to have the opportunity to decide whether or not I should marry Matthew. The real question was should I let this information effect my decision?

"Sarai, please say something." Matthew interrupted my thoughts.

"I apologize, Matthew," I said shaking my head. "I am attempting to make sense of what you have told me. I am unsure what to say."

"I understand. It took me awhile to comprehend it when I first learned of it. I did not know what to do with it. But overtime, I realized that it did not really change who we are. This summer confirmed that for me and I realized that we really need to be seeking God's will for us, whether we are together or not."

That was very helpful. Knowing Matthew had already thought through this and had such a God-centered response was very comforting. "Thank you for sharing. And thank you for being honest with me about your feelings and being open to God possibly doing something different with us."

"It is my pleasure to share with you."

"What you said reminded me of something Mrs. Leland told me a couple of times while I was in the city. She said to consider for God's plan and purpose, would we be better together or apart."

Now it was Matthew's turn to think. I waited for a few minutes before he said, "That is something I have not thought of but a good point. I will pray that God makes it clear if we will be better for Him together or apart."

I nodded. There was another awkward silence. That was when I decided to try an idea on him that I desired to mention to my parents. "Matthew, I am not sure I want my family to be a secret anymore. What do you think about that?"

I could see the internal struggle. "I would feel better if we could discuss it with our parents before making any decisions on that matter."

"That is my intention, but since you mentioned keeping family secrets, I wanted to see what you would think about it."

"I think I understand why you desire to not keep it a secret anymore, but I am not sure it is the wisest idea for us. There is much to lose in our community if we made this known."

"I am aware of this and it is not a decision I would make lightly, because I do not desire for my family to suffer not of their own volition. I was very concerned Josiah was going to cause unnecessary suffering, which I do not believe to be right. I am coming from the ideology, is it being like Jesus to keep care for family a secret simply to avoid persecution?"

Matthew put on his "thinking" face again. "That is an excellent question, Sarai. Thank you for the challenge. I will think about this, though I think I know what our parents will say at this time."

I nodded in agreement. I agreed to give him time to think and pray before approaching my parents about it together. Together? Yes, that is what he asked. During this conversation, I realized I had yet to talk with my parents about what had happened when Josiah returned. I made a mental note to ask Mama about it as soon as possible.

We came to good stopping point, and we decided that it was late enough Matthew should be heading home soon. The family began to come in to prepare for bed. Matthew bid us good night and left for home.

Our family time was wonderful. I had really missed hearing Papa read the Bible to us and hearing Papa pray for us. We all headed upstairs and got tucked into bed. It was a normal family evening and it was beautiful.

CHAPTER 26

I was first in the kitchen the next morning with Mama right behind me. We began to prepare the dough for biscuits and I took the opportunity to ask Mama about Josiah.

"Mama, I realized last night I did not ask you, what happened when Josiah came home?"

Mama stopped. I had asked more than I realized. "It was very challenging." Her voice caught. I saw her wipe her eyes with the back of her hands. "I apologize, Sarai. I cannot speak about this now. I will ask Papa if we can speak with you tonight."

"Yes, ma'am." We went back to making breakfast.

It was a normal Monday the rest of the day. We cleaned up from breakfast, mended dresses and trousers, made lunch, cleaned up, swept the house, worked in the smaller garden, worked on clothes for Josiah's wedding, made dinner, cleaned up, and prepared for family time. I had forgotten how much work we did on a daily basis. I had forgotten how good a day of full work could feel. It was exhausting after three months on vacation, but it was wonderful.

We prepared to go upstairs, but Papa told me to stay in the living room. I twisted the sleeve of my house coat in my hand as I waited for Papa and Mama to return. It seemed to take an hour. Finally they sat down across from me. They were both tense. Mama had a handkerchief in her hand.

Papa leaned forward, cleared his throat and began, "Mama tells me you have inquired about Josiah's return."

"Yes, Papa," I answered quietly.

Papa shook his head. "Except for Papa when Mark left, I have never seen a man so angry." He paused for a moment. Mama wiped her eyes. "He accused us of being traitors and questioned our devotion to God." Mama let out a small sob. "In some way, we almost wanted him to report us to get it all done at the same time. However, we do not believe God wants us to leave and we can be more effective by staying here and still having relationships. I ended up having to forbid Josiah from leaving the house property for a week until he calmed down enough to be reasonable. He has agreed to say nothing to those who do not know for now."

I breathed a sigh of relief, though I only half knew why. "I am thankful to hear this."

Papa nodded. "I do not wish to put undue pressure on you, Sarai, but I think you should know that if you do decide to leave permanently, I may not be able to keep him silent."

My heart raced. This was a twist I was not expecting. "I see. Thank you for telling me."

"It is important, too, for you to have all of the information. But now we all must sleep."

"Papa, may I ask another question of you before bed?"

Papa furrowed his brow a little but answered, "Yes, you may."

"When speaking with Matthew yesterday, he revealed to me the situation behind our marriage arrangement. Was it your intention to give me to him as a repayment for his parents help?"

Both Papa and Mama started with the question, hurt by it. They looked at each other for a few moments, speaking without a word. Mama nodded and they both looked back at me.

Papa cleared his throat before saying, "We are uncomfortable saying that the betrothal was a payment for the help of the March family, though I can understand how it might appear that way. Because of the sensitivity of what we were doing, we needed a way to help assure, when we died, my brother would not be forgotten. After much prayer and discussion, we decided that our oldest daughter would marry their oldest son. I have no good answer as to why we decided that except that is what we believed the Holy Spirit was telling us to do."

My eyes became moist as I listened to Papa's heart. I was so blessed to have parents who loved Jesus and really sought Him. "I understand, Papa. It must have been difficult for you having two sons first and for them to have to wait for Matthew."

"It was. I appreciate you recognizing that. It was at that time I thought we would be found out by the town, but by God's grace people seemed to understand when Mr. March told them they desired for Matthew to marry our first daughter with little question or suspicion. It was never a secret we were good friends, and therefore I believe people assumed it was because of our friendship."

"God really does protect His people, doesn't He?"

"Yes, He certainly does."

"Thank you for telling me about the arrangement, Papa. It is nice to know the truth from you."

"I am thankful we have a good relationship so you may ask. But now I must insist we go to bed. I am tired and I am sure you are as well."

"Yes, Papa." I kissed Papa and Mama and bid them good night. As I lied down, my mind was swimming with the information from the evening, "Papa and Mama prayed about arranging us and still allowed me a way out. Lord, help me make since of this. And if I leave my family will likely face the unnecessary hurt from Josiah, but if I stay, we have the opportunity to plant seeds of acceptance and spare some drama." I now had a lot more to consider.

*****

On Wednesday, I was surprisingly anxious and happy that Matthew would be joining us for dinner and that we would have time to talk. The day seemed to crawl as I did my housework.

As we began to put dinner on the table, there was a knock on the door. I heard Papa greet Matthew and my heart fluttered. We greeted each other as we sat down across from each other. Dinner seemed to take forever. I was excused from dishes again, and Matthew and I headed to the courting table. Thankfully the little ones went outside so we would not have to be as careful with our words.

Matthew prayed for us and there was a clear mutual understanding of what we needed to discuss first. He began, "I have been giving much thought and prayer to your proposition from our previous discussion. Though on one side I understand your position of being open about the relationship with your family, I am not sure that it is the time for that as of yet. I believe it is best to keep the relationship with your family in the city between our families. If the whole of the community needs to know, I believe God will make that clear through our circumstances."

That was music to my ears. "Thank you, Matthew. I am so thankful to hear that God has spoken to you." I looked directly into his eyes and saw a bright light in them. I smiled widely. "I also agree that it is not yet the time." I looked for Josiah and saw he had joined the little ones outside, so I said, "I spoke with Papa and Mama on Monday evening about Josiah's return. I also realized from what they said that it may be best to encourage and speak truth instead of simply telling everyone that we are in contact with those the others have shunned."

It was Matthew's turn to look into my eyes and smile. "I am thankful to hear God has been speaking to you as well. It sounds as if he is leading us in the same direction currently."

I nodded in agreement. In my mind, I thought, *I had not made that connection, but he is right.*

Matthew interrupted my thought, "Now that we have that settled, please tell me more about your time in the city."

"Before I share more of my experience, I also wanted to tell you I talked with my parents about the arrangement and Papa said they prayed over the arrangement and this is what the Holy Spirit led them to do."

"I did not realize that. That is amazing."

"Yes, it is." I waited for Matthew to say something else, but after a couple minutes, I said, "Would you like to discuss the city now?

"Yes, please."

"I would be glad to tell you all you want to know. Do you have any questions you would like me to answer?"

"To be honest, I do not know what to ask. I know you had a bit of a challenge as you compared our cultures. Would you like to discuss that or simply tell me what you did?"

I thought for a minute. "I have a photograph book if you would like to see. I can tell you stories from the photographs."

Matthew looked a little confused but said, "I think I would like to see that."

I had forgotten that he did not know what photographs were. "Please excuse me while I go get the book."

He stood when I did and I hastily went to get the book. He was still standing when I returned. I showed Matthew the photograph book. "See, these are call photographs. They are images that are captured by a machine called a camera. Evalynn made this book for me." I showed Matthew the family photograph on the front. "This is Evalynn," I said pointing to her.

"There is no doubt you are related to each other. She looks so much like you."

"Indeed she does. Everyone who saw us commented about our likeness." I showed him the rest of the family. He seemed very intrigued. "I attended school there for a couple of weeks. That was quite a different experience."

Matthew asked about the school, the classes, the people. It took him a little while to ask about my clothes, almost like he was trying not to. I explained shopping and choosing clothes and told him about my trip to the mall.

"You look so beautiful." It sounded as if he could not contain the words. "The clothes look very nice, yet still modest. I am very surprised by that."

"It was challenging to find modest clothes, but I found a few in which I was comfortable."

The little ones came inside. Our eyes met with a "to be continued" look between us.

We stood. "I will see you on Saturday afternoon. I look forward to hearing the rest of your stories and seeing more photographs."

"I look forward to sharing." I smiled and gave a slight bow.

Matthew left, and I readied for bed.

*****

Thankfully Saturday came quickly and there was nothing else major the rest of the week. I was tired from adjusting back to the normal life but excited for working through the rest of the summer with Matthew. I was nervous to explain all that took place with Austin, but I had been praying that Matthew would be as understanding as he seemed in his letters.

Mama, Tamar, and I had just finished the lunch dishes when Matthew arrived. I greeted him then went to get the photograph book. The little ones went outside to play. I opened to the page with pictures from the pool. He asked me to close it and simply tell him about swimming. He said it sounded fun and expressed that it might be a skill worth learning.

The next few pages were from camp. Matthew enjoyed hearing about the lessons and the beauty of the mountains. I mentally debated whether or not to start the Austin story but decided to tell it all at once at the end. We moved to vacation. There was a page of photographs I took. He enjoyed looking at those. I then showed him mission trip and shared many of the difficult things I learned. Matthew was clearly moved by the stories of fatherless children and confused at the idea that there are other religions apart from Christianity. I wrapped up with the farewell party and the love I felt from those who had gotten to know me.

"You are so blessed to experience so much," Matthew said. "I pray that we might have an opportunity to do something like this together."

"Yes, I hope to go to the city again one day, though in some respects it is difficult knowing there is another way to live."

A silence fell between us. I knew I had to tell him about Austin but how did I begin? Matthew helped me by asking, "I realize this may be difficult, but please tell me about the boy that caused such a stir with Josiah."

147

There came the knot in my stomach. "Yes, I will." There was a knot in my throat. "Before I begin, I want to apologize for my cold heart before all of this took place. It will be difficult for me to tell but I believe it will also be difficult for you to hear. I want to be completely honest with you, so you will know my struggle. Are you all right with that?"

Another moment of silence. Matthew looked at his hands and took a deep breath. When he looked back at me, he had a brave face. "Yes. I want there to be no secrets between us. You may tell me all."

I nodded. I began with my feelings as I left and my perceptions of his family and him. I told him how Austin and I met and the development of the relationship. I explained the letters between us and how they fit into my decisions. I went back to camp and mission trip and the talks I had with Mrs. Leland. This led to my study of this Scriptures on love and marriage. I told him about my struggle of understanding what real love is and how I believed initially the physical was important but now understood why they kept us apart. I concluded with the farewell party and Austin kissing me. I saw Matthew wince and my heart broke as I admitted this. Tears filled my eyes. I could not look at Matthew. I saw his hand on the table.

"Sarai, please look at me." His voice was kind but shaky. I tilted my gaze toward him. His eyes were gentle. "As difficult as this is for me to hear, because it is difficult for me to hear, I knew I had to let you have this experience. I knew you were unhappy before and truly wanted you to know for sure where you belong. I am blessed to have Samuel as a friend, and he helped me to let go so that you could seek God's best." The tears were now flowing. "Please, do not cry."

I wiped my eyes. "You really do care for me." I could barely speak.

"Yes, I do so much." He smiled. "In fact, you leaving helped me to know how much I care for you and I pray I will never take you for granted."

I heard Mama and Tamar come to the kitchen to prepare dinner. I took a deep breath and got myself together. "I should help them. Thank you for your kindness and understanding."

"It is what Jesus does for us." A smile accompanied his words.

"Yes." We stood. I went to the kitchen and Matthew went outside to talk with Papa. I did my best to keep my eyes on my work, but I wanted to look at Matthew, really look at him. I had no idea what we would discuss after dinner now. I supposed that would be part of the growing process of communication.

*****

After supper, I asked if Matthew and I could sit on the porch instead of at the courting table. Papa and Matthew agreed and we settled in two of the rockers. Matthew made sure to put the chairs at an angle so we could still see each other's faces. I stared out into the field. The discussion of Austin had drained me emotionally, and I really had nothing left to share. The silence stayed between us longer than I anticipated. This caused me to look at Matthew who had been staring at the field as I had been. I noticed our hands were close enough we could have reached out and joined them. My gut instinct was simply to do it, but I refrained. This was a new feeling for Matthew that I had yet to experience. I desired to show him affection not in a lustful way, but out of admiration and what I was beginning to discover as real love.

"It is difficult is it not?" Matthew said interrupting my thoughts.

"What is difficult?" I asked.

"The lack of physical affection between us. When you spoke of your realization as to why they keep us apart, it resonated and intrigued me. To be honest, I am envious that you were in a place where it is not shameful to show basic affection. I must fight when we talk to not hold your hand." Matthew and I were looking into each other's eyes. He leaned in, holding his own hand.

I was at a loss for words. "Really?" was all I could manage.

"Yes," he nodded. "We are taught to pretend we do not have such thoughts, but we do, and it is difficult to know how to handle it. I am blessed to have a Papa who taught me how to fight and why it is better to wait for these things. I know it will be that much more special when we are married."

I smiled at Matthew. "Thank you for sharing your struggle. It is helpful to know I am not alone in fighting."

"When I saw you leaving, I wanted to run to you and give you a farewell hug, particularly since I was unsure if you would return."

"You saw me leave?" I was confused.

"I awoke early and walked to the crossroads to think and so I could mentally say goodbye if you did not return."

The tears began to fill my eyes. "I am so sorry that I hurt you and caused you to worry."

"Sarai, I told you previously I wanted you to go so that we would both know what was best."

"How did you let me go like that?"

"Samuel asked me what I would think about you joining Amelia and him in the city, for I could sense you had doubts. After thinking on it, I decided it would do both of us good to have some time apart and get some perspective. It was not easy, but I had peace about it."

The tears flowed. How could he love me like that? He is a much better man than I thought. He risked his own heart and happiness for mine. What is that if not love?

We said little else that evening. Matthew excused himself to go home as we began family time. I listened and prayed silently as Papa read. Things were becoming quite clear. Then Papa read about reconciling and forgiving your brother. I realized then that Josiah and I had barely spoken since I had returned home. This was very odd, and I knew I had to talk to him but did not know when, since Matthew would be back with us the next day and Josiah was also spending a lot of time with Joanna. I knew I needed to spend time with Matthew, but there were other relationships that also needed mending. As I went to sleep, I prayed for wisdom on how to approach the subject and time for it to happen.

CHAPTER 27

At breakfast the next morning, Mama and I had a few minutes alone and so I mentioned talking to Josiah. "Mama, last night Papa said that we are to reconcile arguments with our brothers. I then realized that Josiah and I have not discussed what happened in the city. In fact, we have barely spoken at all. It has been but a week since I returned, but this lengthy silence is bothering me. Will you help me, Mama?"

The concerned serenity on Mama's face startled me. "Your heart is precious, my darling. I will speak with Papa and see if one evening this week, you might be able to speak, but know that Papa and I will be present. I hope there can be true reconciliation between Josiah and you. Be prepared in case it goes poorly."

"Yes, ma'am. Thank you, Mama." I went back to my dough and prayed silently. "Lord, please help us to reconcile. Please open Josiah's heart to Yours that he may love no matter what happens in our family."

*****

After lunch, I insisted on helping Mama and Tamar with the dishes before joining Matthew on the porch. "If this were our home, I would be in charge of doing the dishes. He needs to see me doing my job and know that I take my home seriously."

Mama seemed pleased with my answer and did not argue. Matthew talked with Papa while we worked and I enjoyed watching them while I washed. I tried to read their lips and figure out what they were saying. I smiled to myself thinking about them talking about their fields or animals or something else in the man domain.

When I finished my work, I went on the porch. Papa and Matthew stood to greet me, both smiling. "I will leave you two to talk for a while," Papa said heading inside.

"Thank you, Mr. Lindell," Matthew said. We sat in the same rockers we did the previous night. "I am so thankful to see you are a hard worker."

"I am thankful to be back in a place where work is required of me." I laughed at this.

Matthew was confused. "Is hard work not required in the city?"

"I would not say that, it is simply that their work is different than ours. Remember, though, I was on vacation and so no work was required of me for three months. I did cook when I chose to, but little else."

"What was the difference in their work?"

"Almost everything is different. The house chores are similar, but they have electric devices to help with the chores. They do not cook on fire. The men, though, work outside of the home in different industries. For example, Uncle Mark is a doctor and works in an office, and sometimes in a hospital."

"How do they acquire food if they do not grow any?"

"From farms, like ours, that send food to stores as well as other types of food, that are not thought of here. To be honest, our food is better." We smiled at each other.

"How are their jobs decided?"

"They choose what they want to study, and if they make it through their training, they can get a job in that area."

"They can decide what they want to do. They decide who to seek for marriage. They have a lot of decisions to make in their lives, do they not?"

"Indeed they do. It was very overwhelming hearing all of the decisions they can and do make. I thought I wanted that, but in many ways, it is easier to have it chosen for you."

"I suppose that is true, but if you had not had the opportunity to make a decision so big, would you think it easier to have it decided for you?"

I pondered this for a moment. "No, I do not think I would."

At this point, we discussed what choices we really had where we lived and what life might look like for us. As we talked, we realized how much really was decided already by way of family and culture and decided that for the time being that would be okay. It was clear from our discussion that both of us would potentially like to consider something different in the future.

This caused me to think about Josiah and when we reached a clear stopping point I said, "Matthew, I realized last night there is still a strain between Josiah and me that needs to be discussed. Please pray that this will occur soon and that reconciliation will happen."

"Let me pray now." I saw Matthew begin to reach for my hand but stop himself and hold his own hand. He prayed so genuinely for Josiah's and my relationship that I began to tear up. His love was real and more than I expected. Matthew also prayed for Josiah's heart to soften to God working in different ways, especially in regard to the future. This surprised me but pleased my heart to hear. Not long after this, I went to help with supper and Papa went to speak with Matthew.

*****

Our after dinner conversation was light and brief, but pleasant for a Sunday evening. Matthew prayed for us again before he left for home. I was impressed that he prayed twice in one day for us. I had a few minutes to journal before family Bible reading so I took it.

> *I found today that I enjoy talking to Matthew even about everyday things. I enjoy watching him while he talks to Papa and it makes me smile. As we discussed future possibilities we seem to think in the same way and both of us desire more abil-*

*ity to choose within reason. I am beginning
to think this is more of what love really is: a
desire to be with each other, discuss things
and seek God's best together. During this
week, I have seen that Matthew is someone
I could submit to and respect in God's love.
Is this God's answer for me?*

*****

Tuesday morning, Mama sent Tamar to get the eggs instead of me. As soon as the door closed, Mama took my arm, looked in my eyes and said almost in a whisper, "Tonight you will be able to speak with Josiah. Pray all day and prepare your words well, but also be honest. I do not want this to get any worse, but it can be better to get things out in the open even if it is worse for a time. Papa and I are praying as well."

"Yes, Mama. Thank you." My heart was racing as I went back to my work. I had been praying with ideas floating in my mind but now I needed words. "Lord, give me wisdom."

*****

The day crawled. I tried not to watch the sun, but I found myself looking at it all day long. I had no down time to write or pray alone. I was left to think and pray in my mind.

Finally the time came. The younger children were dismissed to bed and Josiah and I faced each other in the living room chairs. Papa and Mama sat on the sofa to the side. Papa said, "Josiah, Sarai has asked to speak with you and deal with the matter in the city." Josiah barely moved but showed a slight sign of suspicion. "Mama and I are here to help with discussion on both sides." At this, Josiah let out a soft huff. Papa glared at him and became firm in voice. "Our plan is to let you both speak, but we will intervene if needed. This attitude needs to go quickly."

"Yes, Papa." He was only half sincere.

"Sarai, you may begin."

I nodded at Papa and looked at Josiah. I took a deep breath and began. "Josiah, I was very hurt and humiliated by the way you treated me at church and at our family's home. Why did you react that way and treat me so harshly?"

"You were not conducting yourself appropriately. You should not have spoken to that boy. One day and you were already betraying who you are."

"Josiah, I speak with boys here to be cordial. Is there really any difference?"

"Yes. Here a boy knows his place and how to treat a girl appropriately and respectfully. That boy clearly had impure motives and no respect for a girl. His hands were too free."

"I told him our rule, and he stopped. I have been taught well and thought I responded well. You were not there to hear."

"There was no need to hear. Even if you responded as you ought, that boy needed to be taught what respect for girls is."

"What you did was not a respectful response. You embarrassed all of us."

"It was for your good."

"It was good for no one. You hurt us all with your actions."

"Well, then, they should not follow the world."

"I was not following the world. I do not understand why you hate Uncle Mark so much, but I do not appreciate you turning your wrath on me. Please, Josiah, admit that you made a mistake. I do not like this tension between us."

"Clearly, I did not make a mistake. You still chose to, what do they call it, date that boy and almost brought more shame on this family. I knew I should have dragged you home."

"This is really not your business, but I was given freedom to explore where I was led. I might have made a small mistake in that freedom, but who are you to take away what was given me? And even in that freedom, I still chose to come back home. Is that not what you wanted? Why then are you acting as if I have committed a major sin?"

"You have made a good decision for now, but I do not trust you to continue to make good decisions. In fact, I am not sure that I can trust our family's decisions much anymore since Papa and Mama and Samuel all allowed you to be so foolish."

Silence filled the room. I looked over at Papa who was turning beet red and Mama who was white with tears welling. Seldom had I seen Papa angry, but Josiah's accusation had clearly driven him over the edge.

Papa stood after attempting to contain himself for a few minutes and forcefully said, "Perhaps you have missed the teaching in the Word that gives us freedom in Christ to follow Him as He leads. Mama and I knew God was telling us to let both of you go to help you learn this principle. I would rather the mistakes Sarai made that drove her closer to the Lord than the self-righteous arrogance of a Pharisee."

Josiah stood and yelled at Papa, "Then take your family from here and leave this place if it is so offensive to you."

"God has called us to stay here and I will not disobey because it is more convenient."

"Then perhaps I shall follow through with what is right for God's people here and tell all of your dark secret."

"Do you care nothing for your family?"

"I seem to be the only one who truly cares for our family. There is a reason we live the way we do and you have quite forgotten this is the way it is meant to be, separated from the worldly influences so that we might not fall."

Papa breathed heavily but did not respond. Tears streamed down Mama's face. I wanted to go to her, but I dared not move.

Josiah looked at me. "You did well by returning and if you continue to be wise and follow our ways, you may earn my trust once again."

How did I respond to that? Thank you? I will do my best? I said nothing and nodded slightly toward him to say, "I understand." Josiah turned and walked upstairs without another word.

When I heard his feet in the boys' room, I ran to Mama and knelt beside her, took her hands, and cried. "Oh, Mama, I am so sorry. I had no idea he would..."

It was Papa who stopped me. "We know he is not who he once was. Satan has taken hold of him, and I am not surprised by any he said." Papa prayed right then for Josiah and all of us as we moved forward. After Papa finished, he looked at me and said, "Thank you for seeking what is right. Let your conscience be clear and seek the Lord gladly."

"Yes, Papa."

"It is late and tomorrow will be full. You should go on to bed."

"Yes, sir." I kissed Papa and Mama and walked slowly to the stairs. Before climbing them, I looked back at my parents and saw Papa tenderly embracing Mama with a Psalm.

Lying in bed, I thought, *Would Matthew comfort me so gently?*

*****

After supper the next night, I told Matthew of what happened on the previous one. As I spoke, I received my answer. His eyes were so kind and full of empathy. It was clear he was hurting in my hurt and wanted to wipe away the tears.

A week and a half at home and I was almost certain I knew the answer to that plaguing question. Matthew was who God was leading me to marry.

CHAPTER 28

Early the next month, I celebrated my eighteenth birthday. It was a grand party with most of the town attending. It felt odd being so fussed over at home, but thanks to my time in the city, I was able to enjoy it graciously. There was food by the pounds, lots of pies and cakes, great music and dancing. I talked with many and danced with Papa, Mama, my sisters, friends, and cousins. In spite of the strain in the family, I was able to enjoy myself. Joanna and I talked some, but Josiah did what he could to keep us apart. It was painful, but I focused on the others who were there to celebrate. Deep down, I think many were there to celebrate my return.

Before dinner, Papa spoke a few words about me and prayed. I was allowed to eat first and gladly took it. Having spent so much time with Matthew lately, it was odd to sit at a different table as he sat with the men and I with my cousins. We had laughs and talked as we ate more food than anyone should. I ate a piece of my favorite, vanilla cake, and was full to the brim.

There was more dancing, some singing, and fun by all. The party began to wind down as little ones became tired and slowly people trickled home. Matthew stayed until everyone had left. My family went inside, and we sat on the porch.

"That was quite a party, Sarai," Matthew said, looking into my eyes. "Did you have a good time?"

I looked back into his eyes, smiling. "For the most part, I did. Josiah did his best to keep Joanna away from me, but aside from that, it was wonderful."

"I am glad to hear it. You have been through much this year. It was time for you to have some good fun."

I laughed.

We sat looking at each other for a moment. Matthew looked in our window for a minute and quickly looked back. I didn't know why, but suddenly I got butterflies. Before I knew what was happening my hands were wrapped in Matthew's and he was staring deeply into my eyes. My breath caught as Matthew began to speak. "I know this is unconventional for us, but your Papa has given me permission to hold your hands and say this. As we have spoken, I have realized much. I realize how much I need God and where He seems to be leading us. I also realize that even if I had been allowed to choose a wife, out of all the girls in our town I would have chosen you. I want a God-fearing woman who loves the Lord, and that is you. With that, Sarai, I ask you, will you be my wife?"

I was speechless. I had seen proposals on some of the movies I had watched in the city, but they were not like this. I knew my response, but I was so stunned I had trouble getting it out. I took a few deep breaths and finally said with a giant smile, "Yes, I will be your wife."

Matthew smiled broadly and said, "I am so thankful." He reached into his trouser pocket and pulled out a beautiful silver bracelet with sapphires. "Happy birthday, my darling, Sarai," he said, putting it on my wrist.

"It is beautiful! Thank you, Matthew."

"You are most welcome."

I was stunned and grateful he was willing to go beyond expectation and tradition. It was time to plan a wedding. We sat hand in hand discussing our future plans as the sunset. We were ready to begin our life together.

ABOUT THE AUTHOR

Emmie Beth lives in the growing suburbs of Atlanta with
her husband, Jim, and their
nine children following God
wherever He leads. She has
been working on creative writing from a young age and is
excited to share her first book
with you! You can connect with
Emmie Beth on her family blog
at themanormanor.blogspot.
com and on Facebook. She also
writes on childbirthconver-
sations.com where she shares
pregnancy and birthing information, encouragement, and
resources.

CPSIA information can be obtained
at www.ICGtesting.com
Printed in the USA
LVHW041938150920
666053LV00006B/477